YOU MUST CONQUER EARTH

J.N. MORTON

COPYRIGHT NOTICE

First published in the UK in 2021 by J.N. Morton // Leamington Underground
www.leamingtonunderground.co.uk

DEDICATION

This book is dedicated to Christine, who will no doubt be thrilled that she is being mentioned in the same publication that includes the phrase: 'a molten jet of shitty whale sperm'.

BY THE SAME AUTHOR

Quiz Me Till I Fact
ISBN 9798677485862
Pop Culture Quiz Questions On Books, Films, TV and Games

Everyone You Work With Is a Cunt
ISBN 9798665234601
A Needlessly Honest Exploration Into The Dispiriting World Of Work

The typeface on the cover and opening headings is **Dr Kabel** by KELGE fonts. Iconography in artwork licensed via The Noun Project.

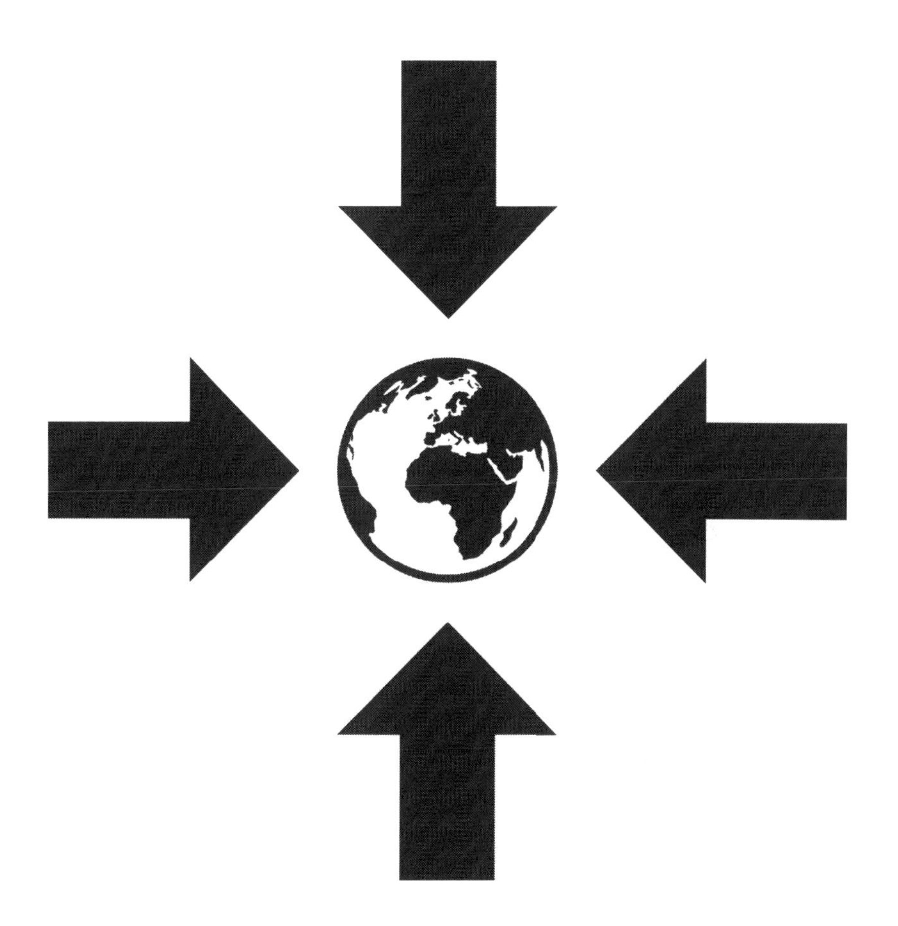

OPERATIONAL INSTRUCTIONS FOR CONQUERING EARTH

1. Begin your conquest on page 5.

2. Use your skill and intuition to make choices, where they are presented *in blocks of italic text*.

3. **Bold text** indicates an instruction to turn to a particular page.

4. Page numbers are at the top of each page.

5. Continue until you conquer the Earth, or meet another ending.

6. Repeat.

5

A SLIMY AWAKENING

Your eye snaps open.

What is going on?

Where are you?

Why can't you move your dorsal tentacles at all?

Why are you submerged in some kind of green slime?

Oh, hang on. That's it. You're in a transport tank.

Yes, you are in a transport tank aboard your hyper-dimensional star-craft, The Pungent Defiler.

A bright blue laser shines through the slime, scanning your dormant body and without warning a voice is transmitted directly into your most dominant brain, "Hutstrog, oollooo ligergret exx polliputolin".

You inwardly groan. The computer is fucked again. That idiot Klurge back at headquarters told you it should be fixed after that whole inadvertent supernova thing a few missions ago.

The voice continues a stream of nonsensical gibberish, "juggggtress kulty tremdop shigfern k k lopred."

By Great Krogon's tail! This is insufferable! You must get this situation resolved immediately.

As you are cased in a slime packed travel tank your physical options are limited, but you are getting a bit of feeling back in your frontal pleasure cavity and you reckon that your minor telepathic gland might have warmed up by now.

If you want to repeatedly dilate your frontal pleasure cavity in the standard distress pattern. ***Go to page 30.***

Or

You could reach out with your thoughts in an attempt to communicate with the computer. ***Go to page 97.***

6

BUY IT NOW OR BEST OFFER

You spend the best part of a CentiCycle setting up an elaborate new online identity, a shady character with the holo-screen ID Painbringr_765 complete with full biographical history and biological marker profiles based on the corpse of a Maskillion Creepstalker you just happened to have frozen in the auxiliary store room.

You create a new Galaxi-web market account for Painbringr_765 and post the Trans-Cosmic Plastic up with an optimistic asking price of two thousand quantics.

As soon as you commit the offer to the market, the holo screen is deluged with hundreds of counter offers, a lot of them are offensively low, but then some serious offers appear from what look like seasoned traders. When an account named Tharg7//Trade4U submits an offer of a thousand Quantics, you immediately approve it.

The Galaxi-web clearing algorithm transmits a secure location for the exchange to take place, just a few systems away. You transmit your approval and plot a course...

The exchange goes off without any problems, Tharg7//Trade4U turn out to be an up-and-coming, quadro-ped, star mining operation who are delighted to get their paws on some high explosives. They handle the transport and credit Painbringr_765's account immediately. They were a pleasure to deal with and you leave them excellent feedback.

Your next stop is at a discreet starcraft outfitter that Tharg7//Trade4U recommended - you are able to get an excellent no-questions-asked trade in on the Pungent Defiler for a Fer-de-Lance class fighter freighter you name The PainBrungr, it's got deluxe fuel scoops and a brand new, blank personality computer. You get them to etch some especially unpleasant Krogan war patterns on the hull and set off for your new life of adventure.

You are genuinely shocked at how smoothly everything has gone.

Go to page 92.

7

WHAT ON EARTH?

"OK, computer," you think in the general direction of the surprisingly useless, meta-quantum intelligence housed in the metal box in the corner, "give me the report on this planet 'Earth'."

"Certainly, Commander," the computer burbles, "Earth is a class three, semi-liquid body and mostly three dimensional according to our instruments. It has moderate bio-chemical resources and some minor trans-cosmic plastic housed in its core-"

"So hardly worth the trip," you interject.

"From a resource perspective perhaps, but it does have a dominant lifeform that might be of use."

"Food or labour?"

"Inconclusive at this point. They are carbon-based and mostly water, so probably quite delicious, additionally their intelligence is shockingly low, so could probably be classed as a cruelty-free product. However their physiology may be suited for basic manual work."

"Right. Well run a deep scan and give me a summary."

The computer bleeps, clicks and whirrs in a way that a hyper-dimensional, gaseous artificial intelligence really doesn't need to (in fact you don't really know why it needs the metal box) and then projects a hologram of two hideous biped creatures onto the deck.

You recoil in horror and involuntarily empty both fear bile ducts across the floor in a surrender pattern. "For Krogon's sake! You could have fucking warned me!" You yell at the computer. "You know bipeds freak me out. Urrgghh. Look at them!"

"Apologies Commander. Would you like me to err, clean that up?"

"Yes and do something about the rest of the mess while you're at it."

"At once."

A trio of tiny drones appear from somewhere and start dematerialising the detritus littering the bridge. The one tackling the sticky yellow puddle of fear bile seems to be having a tough time dealing with it. “Good luck with that,” you chuckle, “I’ve been backed up for at least four OptiCycles.”

Forcing yourself to gaze upon the hideous Earth creatures, you regain composure and ask the computer to give you the basics.

“Although not the most common life form on the planet, these bipeds, are the most dominant and the only ones to score above a point one on the GC civilisation scales for language, communication and technology. Everything else on the planet is pretty much indistinguishable from mould.”

“Wow - that is pretty bleak. So what exactly are… these…?”

“They are known amongst themselves as ‘humans’ or ‘people’. As you have already noted, they are a biped species composed mainly of basic three-dimensional matter and a variety of pre-refinement memetics.”

“Pre-refinement? How on Kellsgratd IV do they score over a point one?”

“It’s an oddity I haven’t seen before. Their civilisation seems to be producing technical and cultural advancements in a completely different order to almost any other recorded example. For instance they’ve never travelled further than that moon over there - but there are many stockpiles of thousands of radioactive missiles, seemingly to use on themselves. Which is… well, it's odd isn’t it? Also they are the only instance I can find in twelve billion planets where the population has invented a planet-wide digital network that they use exclusively for storing two dimensional images of themselves but haven’t got round to unified quantum theory, developing anti-gravity propulsion or even wireless food.”

“Why would they want so many images of themselves when they are so repulsive?”

“I’m not able to form a coherent theory on that with the information that I have so far,” the computer muses. “As we’re on that theme would you like a biological summary?”

“If I have to. Go on.”

“Despite having four limbs, these ‘humans’ are strictly bi-pedal, using the upper limbs and their grabbing appendages for most nonperambulation activities. They have a single electro-meat brain, stored in that growth between the two top limbs, which also houses all their sensory apparatus. Interestingly, despite having two eyes, they can only perceive three dimensions and their understanding of time is entirely linear. A standard human has between two and seven pleasure cavities (available data from their audio-visual entertainment is widely inconsistent on this), which all seem to provide at least one other function."

"Such as what? Actually do I want to know? Is it awful? It's awful isn't it?"

"Well, one is used for communication by expelling gas through it at varying frequencies, as well as ingesting food."

"I.. its... I've never heard anything so disgusting. Really. And I had to deal with repeated outbreaks of Manjaldrian Tentacle Fever on that moon with the radioactive pus volcanoes. Anyway, if their technology is so limited, how on earth do they make new clones?"

"They don't. They reproduce using a manual process that involves-"

"No! No, don't tell me. I really, really don't want to know anything else." You shudder. "And turn off that hologram, it's making me want to perform a total brain wipe."

One thing is for sure, you personally won't be eating any of these dirty creatures - no matter how delicious they may be.

The image of the 'humans' flickers briefly and disappears. You relax slightly and ponder your next move as the tiny robots make tiny noises while struggling to scrub your messy excretion off the floor.

If you'd like to just explode this disgusting, backwards planet from orbit and scoop up any resources. ***Go to page 10.***

Or

If you'd like to plan how to conquer Earth by monitoring their political and scientific activities. ***Go to page 44.***

Or

If you'd like to plan how to conquer Earth by analysing their cultural and entertainment broadcasts - ***Go to page 104.***

IT'S THE ONLY WAY TO BE SURE

You really can't see that Galactic Consolidated would get much use out of these disgusting, backwards, Earth creatures. Even if they are especially delicious. There only appears to be a few billion of them - that wouldn't be enough to provide canapes at the next GC corporate retreat banquet.

A quick comparison of the trending prices of basic slave labour and Trans-Cosmic Plastic leaves you with no doubt at all. The population is entirely expendable and probably more trouble than it is worth - you should explosively excavate the planet core asap.

Unfortunately the Pungent Defiler isn't equipped with mining lasers - huge green beams of light which are the most efficient and aesthetically pleasing way of extracting resources from a class 3 planet. What you have got is a small complement of nuclear inversion missiles, which burrow inside a planet then explode and implode at more or less the same time, effectively turning the target planet inside out. It's a bit messy, but it gets the job done.

The computer targets the optimum locations for the charges and then, with a wave of your dominant tentacle, the missiles are unleashed.

Moments later the Earth judders slightly, goes blurry as all the water on the planet is instantly vaporised and then collapses in on itself, with what you have to concede, is a fairly stunning, spiral shaped pattern. The glowing core of the planet is exposed and begins to solidify in the cold vacuum of space. In no time at all, everything that was the planet Earth now hangs in the void, a misshapen grey-brown lump, its surface speckled with crystalline deposits of freeze-dried Trans-Cosmic Plastic.

In fact, there's far, far more than you could expunge and transport aboard the Pungent Defiler.

If you decide to deploy a homing beacon for a GC mining crew to sort this out and then head back to head office. ***Go to page 12***.

Or

If you want make multiple trips to transport the Trans-Cosmic Plastic to the nearest GC refinery yourself. ***Go to page 16***.

Or

If you realise that this is finally your chance to be rich, load up as much Trans-Cosmic Plastic as you can and sell it on the black market. ***Go to page 17.***

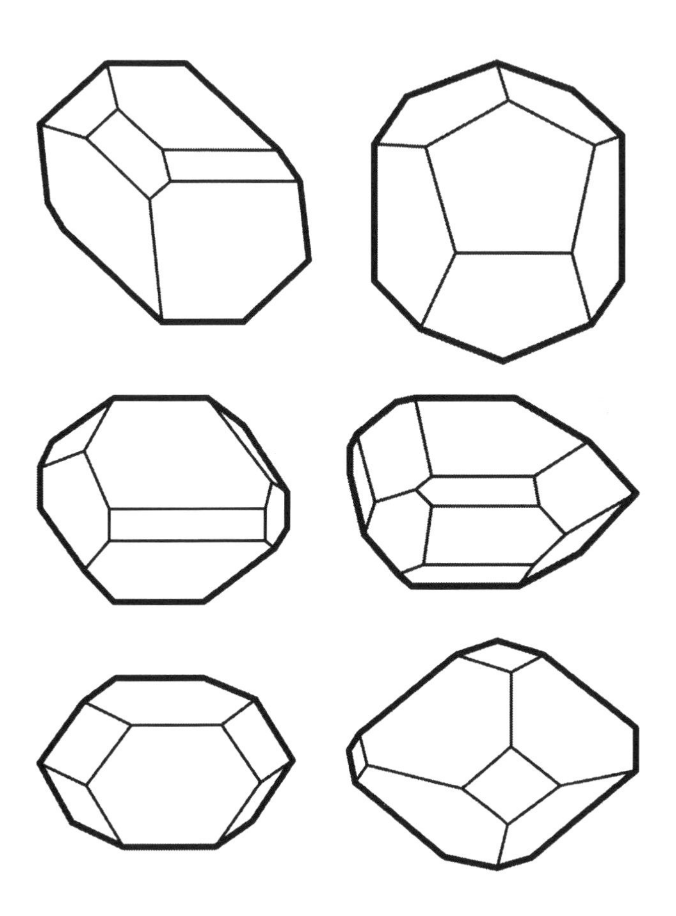

12

THE OFFICE COMMUTE

You didn't spend 8 Cycles at conquering academy to scoop up some rocks, so you deploy a beacon for a GC mining crew to come and salvage the resources from this messy hunk of ex-planet.

By your calculations there should be enough Trans-Cosmic Plastic here to get you a decent bonus and maybe even an increment towards Conqueror Second Level - so not a totally wasted journey. If there's a crew in a relatively nearby system, then the receipt should be in by the time you get back to head office.

You know you should really put any bonus in your cloning pod savings, but it can't hurt to have a browse through the latest GCMart holo-catalogue to see if there are any new brain expanders or pleasure cavity adornments that catch your eye. Hmmm - silicon cladding - that would certainly raise your profile at the next office tentacle orgy.

Right, enough of that, you're getting ahead of yourself. You instruct the computer to plot a low-risk return course to head office and then head to the transport tank, select Aromatic Asteroid transport slime and the third echelon of Gronthor of Claarg's '*Memoir of a World Crusher*' as your travel dream.

Once the slime is at a reasonable temperature, you slide yourself into the tank and begin to enter transport slumber...

Ten hyper-jumps later, the computer revives you (having applied the right brain settings this time) as the Pungent Defiler eases into the docking bay at GC Head Office. You slither towards your local transporter beam station and call up the directory. The map viewer zooms out to show the almost unfeasibly large, dayglo pink cylinder that is GC Head Office, it looks like they added another twelve thousand floors while you were away. Well, things have been a bit slow lately.

Your dominant tentacle hovers over the destination coordinate selector...

If you want to make good on the promise you made to yourself to wreak revenge on that idiot, Klurge, and the IT Department. ***Go to page 21.***

Or

If you want to go and check on your mission bonus in accounting. ***Go to page 28****.*

Or

If you want to enquire whether you have qualified for a promotional increment, make contact with the HR department. ***Go to page 32****.*

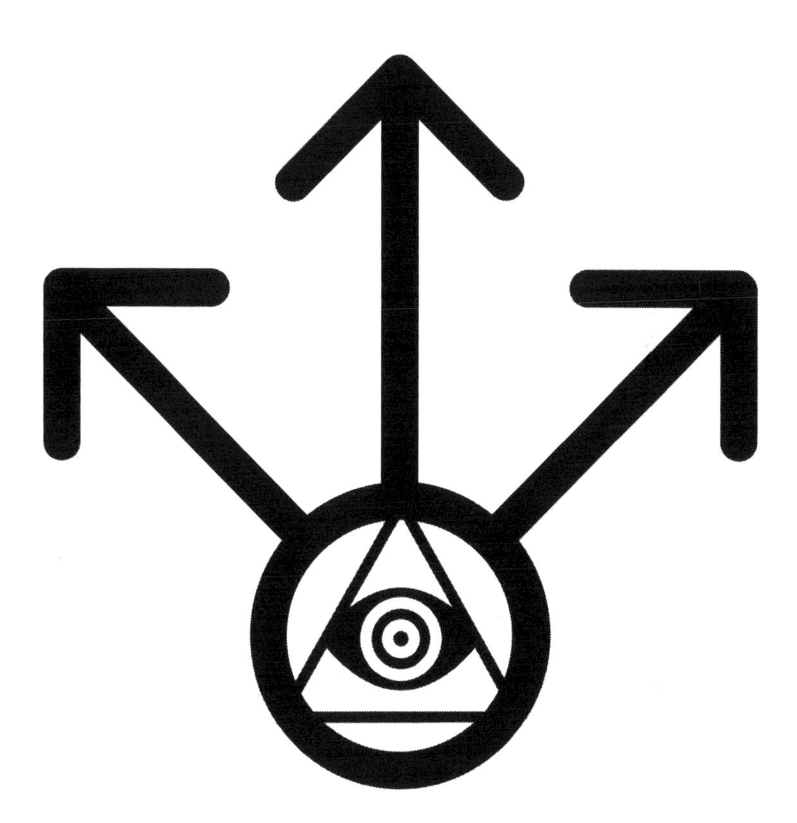

14

DEPLOY THE DARK ARTS

So... there are three main strategic solutions you can employ to render a planet completely enslaved and almost entirely unharmed:

- Exopolitical Theatre

This framework would seem to suit the reasonably organised but devastatingly low intelligence civilisation of these Earthlings. There are two parts, firstly you ascertain exactly who is in charge and strike a secret alliance with them. Secondly, you confuse and bewilder the wider population with a variety of random and mostly meaningless 'alien' encounters and create highly ambiguous evidence of visitors from space. The net effect is that you can be secretly running the planet for the ongoing benefit of GC without anyone knowing - anyone who gets near the truth is thoroughly ridiculed. It's an elegant and self-managing subjugation method, although does take quite a lot of ongoing management and not all resources can be exploited fully.

- The Interloper Technique

Far more risky, but far less resource intensive (which always goes down well when you are subject to a GC Audit), this technique involves you taking on Earthling form and bending the civilisation to your will from within.

You really can't stand the thought of becoming one of these spindly freaks and living amongst them. But you know that your advanced cognitive capabilities - put to work among these single brained monsters - would probably have things tied up in no time at all.

- The Klongrax Switch

This is the sneakiest and the most likely to be successful. This involves you revealing yourself to earth, not as a despotic conqueror, but a benevolent star traveller, throwing yourself on the mercy of Earth to help save your dying planet. You'll throw some anti-conflict memes around and tell them that your race needs a large amount of some basic resource that they have in abundance. In return you'll help them cure a disease or two and maybe even slip them some rudimentary anti-gravity technology. Once they're all set up to help you, a team of more specialist GC operatives will arrive to 'help'. In reality this crew will gradually ingratiate themselves into Earth civilisation and politics and in a handful of Cycles will be running the whole planet as an ongoing GC factory, farm or factory farm.

If you want to negotiate with the secret world government, make patterns in crops and probably mutilate some livestock. ***Go to page 95****.*

Or

If you want to take on human form. ***Go to page 49****.*

Or

If you want to initiate a Klongrax Switch. ***Go to page 135****.*

16

THE FEAR OF (NO) WAGES

From bitter, disappointing experience, you know that any GC mining crew is extremely likely to claim the bulk of any resources recovered from the inside-out husk of the Earth. You'll be left with a tiny proportion of the bonus that all this Trans-Cosmic Plastic should entitle you too.

“Computer, where is the closest GC refinery outpost?”

“There is a devastator class facility twelve systems away, although it is not reachable via hyper jump due to local navigation anomalies.”

“OK, deploy all of our drones to gather as much Trans-Cosmic Plastic as we can hold and then plot the most direct three dimensional course to the facility.”

“But Commander, unrefined TCP is extremely unstable. Any sustained physical disturbance will cause it to explode.”

“So we'd better avoid any physical disturbances then. You have your orders. Deploy the drones at once.”

“As you wish, Commander,” the computer sighs, moodily.

The drones speed off to begin the work of manually displacing the Trans-Cosmic Plastic to the Pungent Defiler's hold, while you glance at the navigation course to reach the refinery. It looks like the ‘navigation anomalies’ that the computer mentioned will make this an interesting trip to say the least...

A few short KiloCycles later and the drones have finished their work. Your ship is now stuffed full of enough TCP to either make you a very hefty bonus, or explosively smear you across the local quadrant.

If you want to spend some time double checking the navigational course that your dodgy computer has laid out and mitigate any risks to ensure your safe and unexploded passage to the refinery. ***Go to page 108****.*

Or

If you are completely confident in the course mapped out by the somewhat moody and eccentric AI that is acting like it might hate you. ***Go to page 47****.*

17

UNDER THE COUNTER SCOUNDREL

First things first. You deploy a small swarm of drones to harvest as much Trans-Cosmic Plastic as possible.

Although the computer warbles something about the danger of personally transporting such volatile and potentially explosive material, it is none the wiser as to your nefarious plans. So as you pop open the system maintenance bay hatch and slither inside, it has no idea that you are about to give it a digital lobotomy.

The system maintenance bay is a small compartment, bathed in red light. The walls are covered in hundreds of illuminated rectangular switches that control the capabilities of the ship and the computer. Why there is a whole room for this, you've never known. It's all very stylish and dramatic you suppose, but whoever decided to make it perfectly symmetrical and anti-gravitational was really taking the piss.

"Computer," you think as boringly and matter of factly as you can, "what is the drone status?"

"All drones back on board and cargo secured Commander."

"Excellent," You think as you disable the computer's quantum communication link and recording facilities with a flick of two switches. For some aesthetically pleasing, but pointless reason, thin perspex slabs move very slowly out of the wall to indicate the subsystems being turned off.

You've successfully blocked the computer from remotely recording and reporting your activities back to GC. They'll notice this and investigate in due course, but with quantum comms being so unreliable these days they are likely to assume a minor failure and wait at least an OptiCycle or so before doing anything about it. You'll be long gone by then.

"What are you doing, Commander?" The computer asks - in a much calmer tone of thought than you would expect. You don't respond. The computer might be partially gagged, but you still don't trust it at all, you need to turn off its higher cognitive functions but leave it with just enough mental capacity to help you pilot the ship.

There are 10 switches that govern the higher cognitive functions, you flip the first three off, to see what will happen. The computer starts singing an old romantic war ballad - you flick a couple more switches.

"Flooge... I can feel it... I can feel my mind going..." The computer croaks weakly. "You bastard," it adds, far less weakly. "You total bastard." The hatch opens and a couple of cleaning drones clutching laser knives swoop towards you.

A clumsy and inelegant gambit: so it must still have some control. You instantly flick off all but one of the switches. The drones immediately turn and head back to their station. The red light flickers and turns blue.

A metallic voice rings out - using actual sound waves, not telepathy "Your computer is running in safe mode - navigation and ship functions available via command console only." Result!

You slither back to the deck, take your position at the console and stretch all of your major tentacles (and some of the minor ones too) with a feeling of excitement and anticipation.

After many Cycles under the yoke of GC bureaucracy You are now the privateer captain of your own old-school, retro, heavily armed space-ship - with a hold full of valuable, if highly volatile, cargo. Adventure and fortune surely await. The first order of business is to offload all this Trans-Cosmic Plastic for a hefty payday.

If you'd like to try and sell a ship full of Trans-Cosmic Plastic over the open galaxi-web to the highest bidder. ***Go to page 6****.*

Or

If you would rather be more covert and head to a shady off-grid planet and sell to a shady off-grid dealer. ***Go to page 67****.*

19

SNITCHES GET STITCHES

You allow panic to ripple across four of your brains while the rest work in parallel to try and find an excuse to get you out of this mess.

"You now have four NanoCycles before Level Five audit commences", intones the auditor, trying not to sound too excited about what they have in store for you.

Your eighth dorsal brain suddenly generates a possible course of action, sends it to three other brains for logical criticism, outcome analysis and personal risk assessment. It comes back with an 86% chance of success. Good enough. You flick out a tentacle and disengage all computer communication methods.

"You now have three-"

"The computer was compromised by an IT upgrade," you blurt with an inelegant mental spasm. "The blame lies with Technician Klurge at head office."

There is a brief pause in the holo-transmission, presumably while they check the veracity of your claim. The computer whirs and flashes angrily in the corner, you click another button to turn its light panel off.

The auditor re-appears, "Commander Flooge, we have confirmed that an upgrade was carried out. You will now be transferred to a waiting suite while a Level One audit is completed."

That's a result! A Level One! The worst they can do after that is demote you to Level Four. The look of disappointment in several hundred of the auditor's eyes is palpable.

"Transferring you to Waiting Suite Five Six Eight now."

You feel the static prickle of a transport beam as the deck of the Pungent Defiler melts away and you slide through a sixth dimensional hyperplane until it resolves back to the three dimensional form of a dank and squalid waiting suite somewhere in the depths of the Audit Department craft...

Nearly three Cycles later, you are still in the waiting suite. It turns out that your computer is some sort of legal genius and has deployed

20

every possible stratagem to delay the continuation of the audit as long as possible.

Time has become meaningless to you. Your brains slip in and out of hibernation mode at random. Your tentacles have started to wither and now and again one of your suction cups falls out - a small pile of them sit in the corner.

Without warning an announcement plays across your battered subconscious: "Due to the extreme length of your audit process, we are rationalising your case's Waiting Suite occupancy to realise this Cycle's efficiency savings. Standby."

The door to the waiting suite slides open and a group of battered and scarred IT technicians enter, led by a very angry looking Klurge.

Regarding you with a cloudy, bloodshot eye, Klurge reaches into their pleasure cavity and retrieves the sharpened chunk of metal that has no doubt been concealed there for quite some time. It glints in the pale light of the Waiting Suite as the IT department slowly close in on you...

Earth Conquering Status: You compressed all of Earth's civilisation to a proton size singularity and then got beaten to death by the IT department in a nasty revenge killing.

Galactic Consolidated Rank: Potential emergency food source, level 4.

The End.

21

THE I.T. DEPARTMENT

As your favourite Materni-bot always used to say: “Revenge is a sweet pleasure best deployed as often and as violently as possible.”

The IT Department have had it coming for some time now, they are as incompetent as they are lazy. The shit with your computer on this trip was the final straw - and that’s after you told them that the ‘database error’ that saw your corporate profile title changed to “Massive Sexual Failure” was the last straw.

You materialize in the large conqueration support atrium and check the local directory to find out where your particular IT subsection is hidden away. As you head toward IT support sub nest 53/q in a most murderous rage, you ping the computer to transport you a small weapons package. A sleek, white plastic tube materializes in the air in front of you, you grab it out of the air and tuck it under your dominant tentacle.

Judging from the noise coming from Klurge’s team workshop, IT management never acted upon the Workplace Termination Recommendation you filed. You slither towards the entrance and consider how best to wreak your entirely justifiable revenge against this gang of annoying nerds.

If you want to sort this out quickly and cleanly in ‘Classic Flooge’ style by tossing an instant inferno grenade into the IT workshop and burning the lot of them to death. ***Go to page 22**.*

Or

If you want to do this by the book and challenge Klurge to corporately approved laser knife combat to the death. ***Go to page 71**.*

22

TURN IT OFF AND ON AGAIN

You fail to see why you should waste your sublime single combat skill on a lowly chunk of tank slime like Klurge - and the rest of the support team are just as culpable for the ongoing disaster that is your ship's computer. Best to burn the lot of them to pieces in the most efficient way possible.

You scan your visual cortex buffer to double check the exact phrasing on the F2/987 Workplace Termination Recommendation that you filed - you don't want to give HR any excuse for one of those ad-hoc eviscerations they are so keen on.

Even this far corner of the conqueration support atrium is fairly busy, but no one is at all perturbed, or even mildly interested at the sight of you pulling a class B inferno grenade from the weapons pouch. You don't get so much as a glance as you set it to 'impact shower' mode and hurl it into the IT support sub nest 53/q office.

As the instant and carefully constrained plasma conflagration burns Klurge and their IT support underlings to a crisp over the course of just a few NanoCycles. Their colleagues slither past, going about their business in a way that suggests to you that vengeful fire-bombings must be a regular occurance in the IT department.

The exact moment that the inferno grenade goes out, a familiar red light begins to flash in this corner of the atrium. The previously calm and nonchalant support staff panic and rapidly disperse as a hole opens up in the floor and the nightmarish, giant, metallic, hideously barbed figure of an HR advisor rises to loom over you.

"Flooge, Conqueror Level three," the horrific automaton thunders at you, "you have perpetrated a multi-victim workplace murder under the extended terms of form 2/987."

There is a brief but terrifying pause before the HR advisor continues. You tweak your pain reduction endorphin gland, just in case.

"Congratulations."

You sag slightly with relief. The HR Advisor gestures towards the smoking IT office with one of its murderous claw arms.

"Your account has been credited with the assets of all of your victims. Due to the variance in rank of your victims, the normal murder-based promotion process cannot be invoked. You will now be subject to an immediate ad-hoc appraisal to determine your continued purpose."

That's a bit of a blow. You hadn't realised that the 'you take what you kill' would apply to job roles in this circumstance. On the other hand, you are now stinking rich.

If you would like to submit yourself to the trial of an ad-hoc appraisal. ***Go to page 75****.*

Or

If you would like to use the hefty stash of money from your firebombing victims to buy your way out of your GC contract, take a brief holiday, maybe check out that weird multi-system sponge collective you've heard about, then buy yourself a new ship, call it the PainBrungr and set out as a rogue-ish privateer seeking fortune and adventure across the known and unknown galaxy. ***Go to page 92****.*

24

BEWARE OF FAILING MASONRY

The left holo-screen shows a group of thirteen cloaked figures sitting around a large, circular stone table. The reception is terrible: static and interference buzzes across the image.

"Can we do something about the reception?" You ask the computer.

"Unfortunately not, all of their broadcast equipment is staggeringly primitive and hidden away under a layer of permafrost. I had to boost the signal significantly to get it this good."

You groan inwardly, but remind yourself that you've chosen this 'Brotherhood of Enlightenment' for their widespread political network, not their technology.

"Brotherhood of Enlightenment," you bellow, "I bid you greetings. I am Commander Flooge, conqueror of many worlds - soon to include your pitiful 'Earth'."

The hooded figures around the table turn in your direction, one of them stands and pulls back their hood to reveal a typically revolting and - from what little you know of their biology - very aged human face."

"I am Gunther Weishaupt," croaks the ancient Earthling, "Grand Prefect of the Brotherhood of Enlightenment and chair of this, the Dark Council."

You consider asking why the leadership of a 'Brotherhood of Enlightenment' is a 'Dark Council', but you know that doing so would be entering a world of tedium.

"On behalf of the Brotherhood, we greet you Commander Flooge and humbly hope that our proposal of cooperation for Earthly domination was satisfactory?"

"It seems agreeable, Gunther Weishaupt, but I need further assurance of your capabilities before we proceed."

Over the course of what seems like an entire CentiCycle, Gunter Weishaupt explains in exhaustive, painful detail the breadth and depth of the Brotherhood's infiltration into the power structures of Earth civilisation.

This lengthy period of establishing subversive power has been known as 'Operation Chokehold' - when The Brotherhood is satisfied that they have a critical mass of power they will then carry out 'The Ultimate Storm' and seize control of the planet.

"Right, well that sounds... comprehensive,' you offer when the ancient Gunter Weishaupt has finally stopped talking. "I'm curious though, what is the timeline for the completion of err, this 'Ultimate Storm'?"

"A mere tick of the clock, in conspiratorial terms," says Gunther Weishaupt, "about one hundred and fifty years."

You glare at the Grand Prefect as he slowly retakes his seat, you can almost hear the creaking of his joints from high Earth orbit.

"Is that an attempt at some sort of humour?" You thunder, "Do you dare jest with me?"

"Not at all, most eminent Flooge, our conspiracy is centuries in the making. Through such gradual methods we have remained undetected through the years and... well... we're not as resource rich as we once were. Are you aware of a phenomenon known as the dot com bubble?"

"Spare me more wearisome miscellania," you growl, dominant tentacle straying towards the lava torpedo buttons on the command console. "If I were able to provide resources and assistance, how quickly could you accelerate your plans?"

"Well it's not that simple, Herr Flooge. We have many plans within plans, subtle intrigues and devious schemes that must play out exactly as planned in order to-"

"Because if you can't come up with a more realistic timescale then I will have no choice but to incinerate you immediately."

"Six months," blurts Gunter Weishaupt, "we could do six months."

You suppose that would be do-able, but for such a lengthy time frame before payback, you'd have to be very tight on the resources deployed.

"Very well, Grand Prefect, that would be just about acceptable. I grow weary of this interminable dialogue and must attend to other matters. Transmit all materials on your requirements at once and I will consider how best to proceed."

You flick off the holo-screen before the old human has time to respond and head off to take care of other matters in the hygienarium.

By the time you've finished and had an extra long steam cleanse, the computer has received and analysed all of the material from the Brotherhood of Enlightenment.

"OK, give me a breakdown of just what these ancient bastards need," you instruct the computer.

"It's not too bad in terms of material resources, a couple of hypno-rays, maybe some quantum comms kit." It responds, "but there is going to be a lot of your time needed. They are looking for a whole mis-direction and distraction campaign, so lots of abductions, plenty of what they describe as 'UFO sightings' and an absolute space-cruiser load of livestock mutilation."

"Oh for Krogon's sake! I thought this would be a chance to have a bit of a break. Maybe work on my memoirs while those hooded primitives did the heavy lifting. Now I'm going to be up to my lateral vents in mind-probe sessions and animal guts. Marvellous."

"Actually commander, I have modelled an alternative."

"Really, what is it?"

"I.. well.. You're really not going to like it."

"You're not going to like what I do to you if you don't explain yourself immediately."

"Yes, of course. Having examined the shortfalls in the Brotherhood's planning, resources and influence, I have concluded that another existing organisation on the Earth could be leveraged in aid of global domination."

"You don't mean?"

"Yes, I'm afraid so - you could get the Brotherhood working with the shape shifting lizards already embedded into the upper strata of Earth civilisation."

"Uggh, you're right - I don't like it. How involved would I need to be?"

"That's the beauty of it, between both groups they should have more than enough power to take over the planet well within the next Cycle."

"So I wouldn't have to actually deal with any of those scaly fuckers?"

"Not beyond brokering some sort of agreement, No."

If you are taken with the computer's cunning plan to combine the collective forces of the Brotherhood of Enlightenment with the (always very annoying) shape shifting lizards and let them get on with conquering Earth on your behalf. ***Go to page 138****.*

Or

If you'd rather provide more traditional support for the Brotherhood of Enlightenment with some extremely cliched extraterrestrial activity. ***Go to page 147****.*

28

YOU DON'T HAVE TO BE A DESPOTIC TENTACLED MONSTER TO WORK HERE (BUT IT HELPS!)

You rematerialise in an enormous, grey-coloured office facility. Hovering in front of you is a sad looking accountant on an anti-grav support cushion, its tentacles withered by too many Cycles spent in the harsh glow of a six dimensional spreadsheet projector.

"Welcome mighty Commander Flooge, I am Countmaster Drex of Accountancy sub-nest B. How may I help you during this NanoCycle?"

"Greetings Drex, you sad and pathetic creature," you bluster, with just the right amount of withering scorn, you don't want to overdo it, always best to try and keep the accountants on side. "I visit your pitiful work enclosure to claim my bounty for the excavation of the planet formally known as Earth"

"Of course. Allow me to transmit us to a nearby meeting room where we can transact this matter away from all this hustle and bustle"

You consider the near silence of the cavernous accounting office and perform a tentacle convulsion to indicate your supreme indifference.

Drex taps a switch on his support cushion and you both rematerialise in a blank white cube somewhere else in the accounting sub-nest. The room is empty except for a small transporter kiosk and a cheesy 3D motivational poster which depicts a small planet being lasered to pieces by giant hyper squids.

The accountant, shudders slightly and winces, it is either telepathically retrieving an information file, or discharging a waste pellet. "So, Commander, according to our files, GC Mining recovered twelve Quantics of Trans-Cosmic Plastic from the planet formally known as Earth..."

"Stop your insignificant babbling, Drex," You snap, as politely as you can. "There were at least two thousand Quantics of TCP on that hideous rock."

"I beg your pardon, glorious Flooge, but the receipt from the mining rig in question clearly states that they recovered and processed twelve Quantics."

Great, you've been completely fucked by the mining department.

Again. Bastards.

Drex senses your anger, probably from the smell of the bile that your rage sacs have just spewed across the walls of the small office. “Would you like me to engage an Audit Squad to investigate this discrepancy, mighty Conqueror?”

You freeze in fear, contemplating the sad little accountant in front of you and the threat of almost certain death that it has just issued. You need to be careful with this one.

“No. That won’t be necessary, Countmaster. Just credit my account with my bonus for the twelve Quantics and I will be on my way.”

“At once Commander, your share of the resources recovered is six Quantics… and you used thirty Quantics worth of Inversion Missiles to secure them.” Drex informs you.

You don’t like where this is going at all. Using your encrypted communication cortex, you ping the code phrase 'Aaaarghhh!' to the ship’s computer, telling it to set a pre-emptive transporter beam lock on your current location and to get the hyper-drive warmed up.

“But the last time I used Inversion Missiles, I was never charged for them, so I assumed that they were complementary for Level three Conquerors?”

“A most amusing and witty thought, Commander, but no, GC Inversion Missiles are not a complimentary item.” Drex intones in an almost threatening timbre. “Your account is therefore in debit to the amount of twenty-four Quantics - I take it you will want to settle this amount at once?”

You both know that you have no way of paying that kind of debt. Your eyes lock across the meeting room, while a team of small automated drones attempts to clear your viscous rage bile off the walls.

If you want to make a break for it. ***Go to page 83****.*

Or

If you want to try and work out some sort of payment plan with Countmaster Drex and the GC accounting department. ***Go to page 73****.*

30

GOOD NEWS AND BAD NEWS

With a great deal of effort you flutter the opening of your frontal pleasure cavity in an attempt to communicate with the malfunctioning computer.

The good news is that your wild dilations do indeed attract the attention of the computer. The bad news is that after a lengthy spell in the travel tank, your muscles are a bit stiff. Instead of signalling a message of distress, the frequency of your dilations actually communicates a serious and non-retractable desire for immediate euthanasia.

The computer is surprised, but having known you a while, not all that surprised. So it immediately begins the process of jettisoning the contents of the travel tank into space.

As you slide, a slime-encased cylinder, into the stark vacuum, you catch a glimpse of a smallish, blue/green planet - probably a class three you think. You would have really enjoyed conquering that, but instead you freeze to death, destined to drift into eternity…

Then your frozen corpse bumps into a corner of The Pungent Defiler and is shattered into a million tiny frozen pieces.

Earth Conquering Status: You died due to inaccurate flapping of your sex hole before you even began trying to conquer the Earth.

Galactic Consolidated Rank: Conqueror, level 4 (posthumous demotion applied).

The End.

31

AN AD-HOC APPRAISAL - ROUND 3

You're not sure exactly why you chose the square and stars, but it seems like it must have been a good choice as the tunnel deposits you in another white cubic room rather than the smelly acid death pit.

A new metallic voice rings out:

"Appraisal Round Three begins now. Please consider the following scenario and choose the appropriate exit."

Two new portals open up in the wall opposite you, one is coloured blue, the other is coloured red.

"During a standard conqueration voyage, you discover that an overly competitive colleague has secreted an explosive sabotage device in your cargo hold. Fortunately you locate the device before it is due to detonate, unfortunately there are only a couple of MicroCycles left on the timer.

The device itself is crude, but cannot be moved or transported without almost certain detonation, the timer is connected to a dark matter explosive by two wires: one is red the other is blue. Which wire will you cut to prevent the device from detonating?

You have one MicroCycle to choose an exit before mandatory de-consitution."

If you want to choose the red exit, because everyone knows that you always, always cut the red wire. ***Go to page 43***.

Or

If you want to choose the blue exit, because everyone knows that you always, always cut the red wire - but because of that the overly competitive colleague in this scenario will have switched the wires to trick you. Of course they might double bluff you by not switching the wires at all, but you don't think that the imaginary colleague would be nearly cunning enough to try something like that. ***Go to page 53***.

32

THE H.R. DEPARTMENT

The prickly sensation of a local transporter beam fizzes and you materialize in the terrifying gothic cavern that houses the Galactic Consolidated Hierarchy and Retribution department. The whole place is a (carefully calculated) assault on the senses.

Hanging from the ceiling is the HR logo: an actual inhabited planet, shrunk down to one millionth of its actual size, in a spiky metal cage. A heavy perfume of Digi-Whale breath overwhelms your olfactory gland and the latest Hypno-Tracks blare out - it's the only way they can keep the smell and screams from the Appraisal Process down to a reasonable level.

You head to a consultation station and an enormous, vicious-looking HR Advisor rises from the ground in front of you, its spiked metal limbs still glinting with the vital fluids of the party or parties from its previous meeting.

"Flooge, Conqueror Level Three. Select a purpose for this interaction: One - Hierarchy Progress Enquiry. Two - Workplace Termination Recommendation. Three - Holiday Allowance Services."

"Hierarchy Progress Enquiry."

The HR Advisor spins all three of its metal death-claws in anger, bits of flesh fly off in all sorts of directions. "You didn't respond correctly", it rages, "you didn't say the number!"

"I didn't know it was required," you complain, wiping a bit of what you assume was a former colleague out of your eye.

As the HR Advisor lets out a howling hexadecimal scream and spins on all four axes, you have a vague feeling that you might be in trouble.

When a silver barbed limb shoots out and severs the tip of one of your favourite tentacles, the feeling becomes more solid. Everything else is becoming much less solid, the severed tentacle sprays green life fluid in a high pressure arc all across the HR Advisor, while your panic sacs squirt fear fluid all over the floor in an intricate deference pattern.

This wet display seems to calm the HR Advisor down a touch, its manic gyrations calm down a bit and a superheated death claw shoots out to cauterize your gushing tentacle. The pain is so intense that you ejaculate a splodge of grey terror slime directly upwards, it hangs in the atmosphere for a brief moment before showering you in dark semi-liquid shame.

“Flooge, Conqueror Level Three, select your purpose before I am forced into further enforcement of our Respect in The Workplace policies.”

“One - Hierarchy Progress Enquiry.” You carefully enunciate, beginning to shiver from shock and massive fluid loss.

“Flooge, Conqueror 3, you have been awarded a single progress increment since your last mission. Select an option: One - Bank this increment for future use. Two - Use this increment to trigger an Appraisal Process.”

While you consider your choice, a team of drones appears, cleans you up, dries you off and applies a new tentacle tip.

If you decide to bank this increment and then take a transporter to the IT dept to sort those bastards out. ***Go to page 21****.*

Or

If you decide to bank this increment and take the transporter to check on your no doubt hefty bonus in Accounts. ***Go to page 28****.*

Or

If you want to take this opportunity to try and get a promotion via self submission to an Appraisal Process. ***Go to page 75****.*

34

LET THE NEGOTIATIONS COMMENCE

As fun as this all is for everyone, you think it best to try and at least negotiate a bit with this bunch of vile bipeds before you blow up anything else. You're not too clear on who or what you should open negotiations with though, you haven't received a single psychic ping of surrender or even a rudimentary pleading holo-transmission. It's starting to look like you might have to actually interact with these disgusting simpletons.

"Right, who, what or where is the main seat of power on this rock?" You ask the computer.

"Hmm," it says, entirely unnecessarily, "The most powerful entity on the planet is a human name 'Myra Eagleton' who holds the position of 'President of the USA'."

"Fine, get this Myra Eagleton on a holo-conference and we can speed this whole thing up."

"Unfortunately Commander, the Earth human Eagleton was resident in the first landmark you so skillfully obliterated."

"Marvellous - you could have mentioned that."

"Apologies, Commander."

"Ok, so who is the most powerful post-Eagleton?"

"That would have been Igor Nastovich, the 'Premier' of a rival state called 'Russia'."

"I'm noticing your use of the past tense."

"Er, Yes."

"We've melted that one too haven't we?"

"I'm afraid so."

"So where does that leave us?"

"Well the humans do have a sort of planetary council known as 'The United Nations'".

You groan, "Ok well put me in touch with them, I suppose."

"One moment, Commander… There, you should be in audio visual conference with what they refer to as The General Assembly in a couple of NanoCycles - I've adjusted instruments for psychic to sound wave translation."

The holo screen flickers and resolves to the image of a large room filled with all sorts of the vile earth beings, sitting in semicircular rows, all looking up at you. Presumably you are on some kind of screen at their end as a number of them flail their limbs around in celebration at your appearance, some of them even seem to be so impressed by your tentacular magnificence that they expel copious amounts of fluid from the weird hole located beneath their eyes.

You set the audio configuration to maximum intimidation and address the cowering primitives:

"United Nations of planet Earth - submit immediately to the rule of I, Flooge, or condemn yourselves for summary obliteration."

One of the humans rises, and begins to blow soundwaves through the hole that they had just been purging chunky fluid through. Disgusting.

"I am the Secretary General. First let me apologise for all the vomiting. Your, err, appearance seems to have caused quite the reaction amongst our delegates.

We, of course, wish to avoid further destruction and loss of life and have no choice but to agree to the immediate surrender of the Earth."

"Excellent," you boom.

"We just have to pass a resolution first."

"And how long will that take?" You ask, a stray tentacle lingering near the death ray button.

"No time at all," the secretary general assures you...

Three Earth 'weeks' later you open the connection with the United Nations for an update on the surrender discussions.

"Secretary General, are you now, at last, ready to formalise the terms of your planetary submission?" You thunder.

"Very imminently, Commander Flooge," replies the vile human, "We just need the final risk analysis report from the surrender sub-board to be ratified by the Assurance committee. Then we'll be ready for a full vote on the main resolution"

You glower, "My understanding was that such a ratification had already been attained."

"No, no, no," chuckles the Secretary general, "That was merely the business case for the formation of the research panel."

"Oh, right, yes , of course, well, hurry it up will you? My patience is wearing thin, Secretary General."

"Of course, I will ensure the members of the liaison committee are taking all measures necessary to expedite all compliance procedures." The secretary general says in that amazing dull and placatory tone - if you didn't know better you'd say that his disgusting human features are looking quite pleased with themselves.

You snap off the holo-conference and consider your options:

If you tire of this obvious Earthling subterfuge and time wasting and decide to simply lay waste to this bureaucratic nightmare of a planet in a devastating display of destruction in order to mine any valuable resources. ***Go to page 10.***

Or

If you want to play the long game and allow the humans to finish their petty, organisational wrangling so that you can quickly and easily subjugate the population without too much fuss. ***Go to page 61***.

37

A VULGAR DISPLAY OF POWER

There's only one thing that all primitive species respect (well there's two, but you don't have any Dancing Sex Trees with you on this trip) and that is a needlessly excessive example of destructive power.

You need to leave these puny simpletons in no doubt of the kind of burning acid terror-death that you will rain down on them if they don't do exactly what you tell them.

You plunge the Pungent Defiler into the planet's atmosphere, fly around the Earth for a bit, just to be sure to whip up a bit of tension and fear. Then, hacking into all communication frequencies used by the Earthlings you deliver standard conquering address 12/1.3:

"Earthlings of Earth. I, Commander Flooge command your immediate subservience to the corporate objectives and tactical whims of Galactic Consolidated. The terms of your immediate surrender are absolute and any resistance will result in your obliteration. It is my duty to inform you that your obliteration may be recorded for training purposes. I will now demonstrate my ability to rain awesome destruction upon your pitiful civilisation. Please have whatever passes for your planetary leadership ready to signal your complete surrender once the demonstration is complete."

So, just what sort of vulgar display of power will you choose to engage in?

If you want to blast a limited number of the Earthling's landmarks with the good old Death Ray. ***Go to page 145****.*

Or

If you'd rather set an example via the terrifying plasma bombardment of a an unpopulated area. ***Go to page 41****.*

38

NEBULIZER!

You wince as you exit from the right hand temporal rift, hoping that if you do go back in time that you remember to pay more attention in the clone enrichment tanks this time and not to give up learning the OctoThrumuliser so young.

Fortunately, you seem to have chosen the correct option, or at least the one that seems like the most correct option, I mean, if you can remember being in the temporal bubble moments ago, then you must have chosen the correct option. You'd ask the computer but it is still defragging (the readout says 89%) - so you just decide that everything is ok, or at least as ok as it can be.

It's not far to the refinery now, but your instruments indicate that there is one final hurdle to overcome - the refinery is located within a fifth tier, gas cloud nebula.

This shouldn't be a problem, the computer will be able to overcome the physical and electronic navigation blackout caused by the nebula by using meta-dimensional geometry. You glance at the readout, the de-frag is still at 89% - the wavy holographic progress bar isn't moving forward at at all. You bring the ship to a full stop on the perimeter of the nebula and decide to grab a snack while the de-frag process finished off...

Three OptiCycles later you awake from a short nap amid a small mountain of food containers, you side-blink some eye crust away and fix on the holo screen readout. It's still on 89%. If you hadn't had ninety percent of your tear glands gelded, you could weep, you really could...

Another six OptiCycles later and the progress bar is, of course, still locked, pulsing slightly, at 89%. Your food stocks are beginning to run very low, the materializer could make more, but the computer has to be running for it to operate safely. You know of at least three other conquerors who have maimed themselves for life by trying to manually operate a materializer. Grruut from sub-section eight was fully bisected while trying to make breakfast.

You decide that this whole thing is a dead loss and manoeuvre away from the nebula so that you can suffer the horrendous indignity of having to contact a GC support crew to come and sort things out. As you try to start the engines, the default ship voice announces: "An engine restart without computer oversight requires your password. Please recite it now on the main psychic band."

"Flooge1234," you think, as loudly as possible so that it will be picked up by the ship's basic psychic plug in.

"Password Flooge1234 ...... Not accepted," responds the ship.

"Flooge_1234," you think instead, fairly sure that that is right.

"Password Flooge_1234 ...... Not accepted - you now have one password attempt remaining before mandatory-"

"Oh fuck off!" You think, possibly a bit too clearly.

"Password Oh fuck off ...... Not accepted - as per warning manadatory self destruction is now enabled - commencing in 15 nanocyles. 14. 13..."

Well, that's just marvellous isn't it? Just fucking great. As the potential final few moments of your life tick down, you speed your perception up to maximum to slow down your subjective experience of time and try to think of what to do.

"Tttwwweeeelllllvvvvee," says the ship.

You are really starting to regret selling the escape pod to pay for that mini-break to the slime pits of Kelkovian Minor.

"Eeeellleeeeevvveeeeeeennnnnn," says the ship.

You could risk bringing the computer back mid-sentience de-frag, although that could just as easily cause something terrible to happen.

"Ttteeeennnnnnnnnn," continues the ship.

But as you are about to blow up anyway, how much worse could it be?

"Nniiiinnnnnnneeee," insists the ship.

You do a quick calculation as to whether you could fit in a final high speed wank. It would be touch and go, in more ways than one.

"Eeeeiiiiiiigghhhhttttttttt," slurs the voice of the ship.

Fuck it, you're going to have to try to bring the computer back.

You stare at the options below the glowing progress bar, there are three buttons the first is ‘Cancel’, the second, which is helpfully greyed out so you can’t click on it, is ‘Help’ and the third says ‘Abort’.

“Ssssseevvvvvvvvvveeeeennnnnnnnnn,” says the ship.

If you want to click on ‘Cancel’. ***Go to page 59****.*

Or

If you want to click on ‘Abort’. ***Go to page 64****.*

41

BLACK HOLE SUN

It seems likely that showing a touch of mercy to these ugly brutes would go some way to gaining their obedience and maybe even their trust.

You slap a few buttons on the command console to bring up a targeting reticle and add a population density overlay. You rule out blasting one of the oceans as that might set off a far larger disaster than you need at this point and as scans show that there is aquatic life on this planet, you might kill something with some actual intelligence.

You settle for a sparse looking bit of territory in the middle of the landmass that, the computer informs you, the vile Earth creatures call 'Southern Europe'.

As the plasma cannon warms up, a small notice pops up on the screen that there is a substantial subterranean structure in the target zone. "What is that?" You ask the computer.

"Most likely the archeological remains of an older and more basic Earth civilisation, the planet is littered with them. They can't seem to keep a consistent organisational structure going for more than a MegaCycle or so."

"So nothing they are going to miss?"

"It is most likely that they don't even know it's there."

Once again you almost feel embarrassed for the inhabitants of this Earth and hope that they are indeed very tasty - as it looks like they don't have much else to offer.

Just to really make sure that they get the point you make a further announcement, you add a bit of sinister reverb this time, theatricality is an oft-overlooked ingredient in any successful subjugation: "Earth creatures, observe this demonstration and accept that I, Commander Flooge hold your destiny within my many tentacled grasp..."

You flick one of your many tentacles out and click the firing button with a sucker - red plasma heat instantly obliterates a reasonable chunk of this 'Southern Europe' into a sea of molten rock. The death estimator on the holo-screen flashes up '2,800,400' - Oooh, that's a bit more than you intended, but you don't get to be a level 2 conqueror without at least a few micro-genocides.

"Hmmm," says the computer, in a way that you are just certain is going to lead to something bad.

Down on the now molten rock part of the Earth's surface a neon coloured circle is beginning to glow extremely brightly.

"I think that you may have just fired superheated plasma into a quantum well."

"What?" You exclaim. "How?" Your tentacles flashing across the console to fire the emergency thrusters.

"It seems that the subterranean structure you destroyed was a primitive form of dark gravity flange - not that the Earth creatures knew what they had built - they called it a 'particle accelerator'."

The glowing yellow circle begins to expand and drag the surface of the planet in on itself. The Pungent Defiler is barely moving away from the nascent (and incredibly rare) White Hole that you inadvertently created. You increase thrust to 'Maximum Panic Burn' but it makes no difference.

As you, along with the Earth, it's star system and a couple of other nearby stars are sucked into the glowing, quantum abyss of the White Hole, your experience of time slows down to such a degree that you spend a period longer than the lifetime of the universe being crushed into sub-quantum oblivion.

It really, really hurts.

Earth conquering status: Your careless showing off led to the creation of a mostly theoretical cosmic anomaly which crushed you to death over a subjective period of time so long as to be statistically indistinguishable from infinity.

Galactic Consolidated rank: Conqueror, level 4 (posthumous demotion). Your clone batch group was paid royalties from the workplace safety training materials that you inspired. So that's nice.

The End.

43

ASCENDING THE SLIPPERY ANTI-GRAVITY LIFT

After flying round a few twists and turns you are blown from the exit tunnel into a circular, grey adjudication room. The tunnel portal closes behind you and the room shudders slightly, but you haven't started falling into a pit of acidic doom, so it can't have gone that badly.

"Flooge, Conqueror Level Three. Congratulations! Your choices have been deemed satisfactory and you are hereby promoted to Conqueror Level Two point Five. Successful completion of this Appraisal Process has settled any credit issues and supercedes any disciplinary action instigated by the HR or Audit departments. Stand by for transport."

A tickly transport beam flashes and you find yourself back on the deck of the Pungent Defiler.

"Commander Flooge on Deck!" Announces the computer, possibly sounding a bit surprised.

"Congratulations on your promotion to Conqueror level two point five, Commander, you must be very proud."

You do feel a sense of pride, you want to stand here and drink in the feeling of reaching the exalted ranks of level two through the difficult trial of an HR Appraisal Process. But instead you rush to the hygienarium to explosively defecate with profound relief.

Earth Conquering Status: You were able to turn your reckless approach to the conquest of Earth into a glorious triumph by surviving a Galactic Consolidated Appraisal Process. More adventures no doubt await. Once you have cleaned yourself up.

Galactic Consolidated Rank: Conqueror Level 2.5

The End.

THERE'S MORE HERE THAN MEETS THE (SINGLE) EYE

Just as you decide that a quick scan of Earth's political and scientific capabilities would be the best way to proceed, an almost imperceptible tear in the fifth dimension floods your internal sensors for a moment and then disappears. That was weird, like a temporal shift, or causal rift, or maybe you're just hungry.

"Computer," you think, "give me a poli-sci rundown of Earth activity and get me a box of those Xanther Brain Kebabs if we've got any left."

One of the Pungent Defiler's tiny robots shoots out from its hidden recess clutching a foil wrapped package which you gratefully pluck open with a sucker. The computer plays an info blast at your fourth brain while you wirelessly transport a couple of kebabs into your gurgling nutrient sac.

This 'Earth' and its horribly primitive inhabitants (you decide to call them 'Earthlings', that seems original) may indeed turn out to be a bit more unique than you'd expect. Their unusual technology preferences, disgusting physiology and bizarrely rigid, yet unstable political structures may actually make them both mildly useful and easily controllable.

Maybe you could turn Earth into some sort of factory planet/hunting reserve - mixed use colonisation is all the rage at the moment.

Your minds are mostly made up, the population is probably more valuable to you than the physical resources of the planet alone. This will need to be an enslavement conquering, but how best to proceed?

If you want to cower the Earth into submission with a vulgar display of power. ***Go to page 37****.*

Or

If you want to use your subtle skills of manipulation and persuasion to enslave these 'Earthlings' (you really do like the ring of that). ***Go to page 14****.*

Or

If you want to think about it further and realise that the Earth creatures and their no doubt disgusting civilisation could be a viable revenue stream, but they are almost certain to be more trouble than they are worth. Do you really want to spend ages dealing with them? No, you don't - let's just blow up this thing and go home. ***Go to page 10**.*

AN AD-HOC APPRAISAL - ROUND 3

The next room you are transported to is a bit of a shock. Rather than the gleaming white cube you were expecting it is a real mess. Unpleasant brown matter is smeared across the wells and ceiling, while the floor is littered with tiny, sharp, black rocks and a number of putrid, yellow puddles.

You turn down your sense organs to avoid passing out from the fumes.

Two exits open in front of you, the first is labelled with a glowing ‘A’, the other labelled with a similarly shiny ‘B’.

“This chamber was recently populated with a small herd of Arachnovoids,” announces the still very friendly voice. "Based on the physical evidence left behind , did they use this space for A, a bout of ritual combat, or B, an extended Arachno-orgy?

You must choose your exit within one MicroCycle, after which the Arachnovoids will be released back into this space.”

You’re going to have to take a wild guess here, to even the most trained eye, Arachnovoid combat and sex are almost indistinguishable - and you definitely don’t want to be here when they are let back in - you’d rather get slowly melted.

If you guess that the yellow puddles on the floor might be Arachnovoid blood and this was the scene of a fight and therefore go through Exit A. ***Go to page 87***.

Or

If you think the sharp black rocks might be Arachnovoid ejaculate and there has been some sort of disgusting bug orgy in here and therefore go through Exit B. ***Go to page 53***.

47

NEVER TELL ME THE ODDS

The computer might be a bit touchy, but it is a hyper-dimensional genius and almost certainly doesn't want to get blown up either.

"Ok computer, let's go," you think. The Pungent Defiler's thrusters rumble into action as you set off towards the refinery. The journey isn't going to take quite long enough to make it worth getting into the travel tank, but it's still quite a long haul. You decide to spend a bit of time in the comfort of your anti-grav holo-lounge - there are a few new episodes of '*Non-Simulated Matri-Clones of Glaaaarp*' that you haven't immersively experienced yet.

A short while later and you are floating around in the middle of an argument between Matri-Clone 265 and Matri-Clone 341 over who invited who to the annual prisoner melting ceremony. You notice a sudden mild, but impactful shudder. Neither of the Matri-Clones seem to notice - "That wasn't part of the show," you think, "something hit us!"

You burst from the lounge back onto the deck to find the holo-screens packed with chaotic rocky chunks. Oh fuck.

"I know what you are thinking," exclaims the computer, "but this asteroid field isn't quite so dense in any navigational charts or bulletins."

"I don't care," you snap, "another impact like that and the TCP is certain to explode."

"Yes," says the computer, skillfully spinning the ship between two particularly pointy asteroids, "I am fully aware of that."

To be fair the computer is doing a rather good job of navigating the asteroid field - if you weren't so terrified you'd probably be impressed.

After a while things settle into a pattern, the computer pilots speedily around the space rocks, using the occasional laser blast to clear away any small, unavoidable debris. As the asteroid field becomes even denser the computer's maneuvers become more extravagant and risky.

"Stop showing off," you think at it.

"I'm not showing off," huffs the affronted computer, pulling a tri-coaxial barrel roll around a large asteroid before performing a Galaxian inverse swoop between three more.

"Don't get cocky!" You shout, telepathically.

"You may have noticed I'm really busy right now, saving us from certain death," says the computer, "please don't distract me".

It launches into a 760 degree mega-spin and reverse thrust through a rocky gap barely big enough for the ship to fit through. You involuntarily ejaculate fear fluid all over the floor (and some of the ceiling).

If you want to let the computer carry on navigating the asteroid field in the manner of an intoxicated delivery star pilot. ***Go to page 54**.*

Or

If you want to deploy the tactical manoeuvre hammock and finish getting through the asteroids yourself. ***Go to page 57**.*

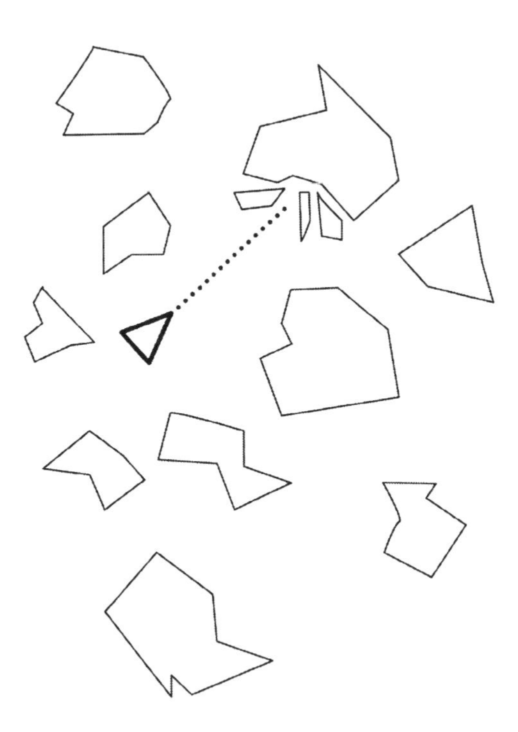

49

CHARACTER SELECTION SCREEN

You really need to try and keep the costs down on this one, you're already in trouble with the accounts dept after the repair bill incurred while pacifying that planet of surprisingly resourceful hedge monsters.

The thought of living amongst these grotesque Earth creatures fills you with violent nausea, but the prospect of an efficiency bonus makes the vile prospect marginally more palatable. You heard that Ooorth from Section Y5 got promoted straight to level 2 and got a brand new ship, all because they managed to completely conquer an entire planetary civilisation by doing nothing more than disguising themselves as a philosophically persuasive and highly talkative cloud.

The Earthlings, backwards simpletons though they may be, are not primitive enough for such tactics, you're going to have to get your tentacles dirty on this one.

"Give me a probability analysis of interloper scenarios and recommendations," you command the computer.

For no reason at all the lighting on the command deck strobes rapidly through a dozen shades of red and the computer issues some low pitch beeps before answering. You really are getting sick of this.

"Only two scenarios both return an acceptable probability of success. Firstly a 'Classic Top Down' option, in which you take on the role of the most powerful creature on the planet - an Earthling named 'Myra Eagleton' who is the leader of the geo-political grouping named 'America'. Secondly - and only barely reaching acceptable probable success - is a 'Slow Burn Subversion' scenario where the target for replacement is an Earthling named 'Kelvin Rust', a famed industrialist, who my temporal projection assessments indicate wil have a hugely significant impact on the near future of the Earth civilisation."

Images of the two repulsive candidates appear on the holo-screen, the sight of them makes the more sensitive parts of your digestive system convulse horribly. You struggle to tell them apart at all. One of them definitely looks far more smug though.

"To be extremely, unambiguously clear," says the computer, "My strong recommendation is to select the Classic Top Down option and take on the form of this 'President of America', the Kelvin Rust alternative is far less likely to succeed".

To emphasise the point, a number of flashing arrows surround the image of the hideous, but less smug creature on the left, while the other one fades out slightly.

If you accept the reasoned, logical approach suggested by the computer and decide to take over the personage of the all powerful leader of 'America', Myra Eagleton. ***Go to page 79****.*

Or

If the increasingly eccentric and annoying behaviour of the computer is making you concerned that its analysis may be flawed and you'd rather inhabit the being of the smug and hideous Earthling, Kelvin Rust. ***Go to page 123****.*

51

DIE PUNY... OH

Right, this really shouldn't take long - looks like a classic 'Burn, Churn & Turn' scenario: widespread destruction followed by deployment of a few AI enslavement drones and maybe a nanite resource stripper if you've got one knocking about in the store chamber.

Switching the Pungent Defiler into 'Withering Offense' mode, you slither into the new tactical manoeuvre hammock you just had fitted and speed toward the unsuspecting planet.

The computer superimposes major population centres onto your view of Earth, based on population levels and technology density - or at least what passes for technology on this rock. Even that planet of semi-sentient sludge puddles you turned over a few Cycles ago had some rudimentary planetary defences, this lot have nothing at all.

Plunging through the surprisingly dense atmosphere you manipulate the strings of the hammock to bring you to rest over one of these pitiful 'cities' for a closer look. Ugh, it's full of creepy, little bipeds, scuttling about with weird jerky motions. Yuck. You've always had a terrible phobia about anything with less than seven limbs.

Rather than look at these disgusting primitives a moment longer than necessary, you unleash a barrage of irradiated plasma and instantaneously reduce the whole site to a scorched crater.

After you've disposed of a few more of Earth's largest cities, they finally show some sort of resistance. A whole load of hilariously basic flying machines have arrived to presumably attack you, which they attempt to do by - and this is so pitiful that you are almost embarrassed for them - firing tiny pieces of metal and small explosive charges at you.

You wipe out the first few groups with psychic shock blasts and then give the new gravity displacer a go and hurl a few hundred of the flying craft in the direction of the nearest star - just to see what they'll do. Not much it turns out.

This is getting dull so you launch a fighter drone on remote and engage in a bit of old-school laser combat with these hapless simpletons. Sometimes it's good to get back to basics and really take your time destroying a planetary civilisation, even one as puny and worthless as this.

Your drone strafes through the waves of Earth's laughable defences, each laser blast cutting through them like a nano-blade through hypno-curd. You notice that the flying machines actually contain the earth creatures themselves, sometimes tumbling out of their stricken craft and plunging towards the planet surface. You start a new game of trying to shoot the flailing limbs off the ones that still seem to be alive as they fall - this is so much more fun than you were expecting!

"Excuse me, Commander Flooge," says the computer, putting you right off a complicated three-in-a row shot you'd just lined up.

"Not now," you grumble, settling for using the magnotron to smash a few Earth craft together in a fiery ball of wreckage.

"But... but.. Commander... I'm picking up radioactive signatures closing in surprisingly fast."

The tactical display switches to show a group of needle shaped objects converging on the Pungent Defiler from a variety of angles.

Oh. That's not good.

Some time later, your horribly burned and damaged carcass is being slowly and painfully dissected by a group of hideous earth creatures. A tiny remnant of consciousness in the anterior cortex of your third backup brain wonders exactly what kind of backwards, fucked-up species manages to invent radioactive weapons before they've even colonised a star system or two. Scary.

Earth Conquering Status: You got distracted while toying with an inferior species, who then nuked you, cut you into small pieces and stored you in eight hundred separate jars.

Galactic Consolidated Rank: Conqueror, level 3 (Missing in action).

The End.

53

YOUR EXCITING NEW OBJECTIVE IS TO DIE

You fly from the portal tube into a grey circular adjudication chamber to receive the result of your appraisal, at least you would if there was a floor.

“That’s strange,” you think as you plummet towards the doom of the de-constitution pit, “I really thought I’d nailed that.”

You have just enough time before you land in the acid lake to massively reduce your cognitive perception so that your slow agonizing, screaming death passes for you in a vanishingly brief spasm of agony before you die.

Earth conquering status: Your efforts to conquer the earth led to all manner of workplace issues which in turn led Galactic Consolidated to assess your suitability for continued employment. You can’t have done too well as your appraisal ended with you being melted down for clone batter.

Galactic Consolidated Rank: Liquid genetic material, level 2.

The End.

54

TEMPORARY INSANITY

There's really no quick and easy way to switch to manual control without risking a catastrophic explosion related event at this point. All you can do is stand there frozen with fear until your idiot computer gets you out of the asteroid field, or splatters you all across the local star quadrant.

After a few more semi-suicidal piloting tricks, the asteroid field rapidly thins out until suddenly you realise that the ship is in clear open space. You attempt to jump for joy, but find that you are stuck to the floor by congealed fear fluid.

"Asteroid field cleared, Commander," announces the computer, fairly needlessly. "Shall I summon a drone to err, clean you up?"

"Yes, at once," you scowl.

The small cleaning robot appears from somewhere to come and scrape up your latest excretions. It makes a small, sad noise and gets to work again. Once your tentacles are free you slither to the command console.

"Computer, begin a full sentience defragmentation on yourself."

"But that will take me offline for a number of MicroCycles."

"I am completely aware of that, I will pilot the ship in the meantime."

"If you say so", mutters the computer. There is a loud click and then the factory default voice announces: "Your computer is now in sentience defragmentaion mode, please do not disconnect power, perform any quantum maintenance or ask any complicated questions until the process is complete or your device may be rendered into an unreachable dimension."

After a quick check of the proposed route you manually re-align the ship and engage full thrust. Chastened by your recent dice with death you switch the scanners to specifically warn you of any forthcoming physical objects. Everything looks clear as you speed on towards the refinery.

The miniscule cleaning robot has nearly finished getting the last of your fear ejaculate off the ceiling and the holo screen reports that the computer is already 33% through its sentience defrag. So in no time at all you'll have a nice clean ship and a far less mentally independent computer, all ready for a nice stress free journey to exchange your cargo. With any luck you'll be able to get back to the '*Non-Simulated Matri-Clones of Glaaarp*' - it seemed like things were about to kick off big time.

You feel a small, worryingly familiar twinge in a couple of your temporal sensitivity glands. You ignore it and hope it is just a small time schism, you do get them around asteroid fields occasionally.

The twinge grows into a dull ache, this isn't just a small schism, you are somewhere near a full on temporal bubble. And everyone knows what that means…

"WHO DARES ENTER MY DOMAIN?" Booms the huge psychic voice of a Temporal Deity. The physical space surrounding the Pungent Defiler transforms into a rotating, five dimensional crystal structure.

By Great Krogons huge swinging balls! You really don't need this.

"WHO DARES ENTER MY DOMAIN?" The voice repeats, "DECLARE YOURSELF!"

Usually you'd get the computer to interact with any Gods that you are unfortunate enough to run into, but as it is only now 40% through its de-frag, you'll have to deal with this pretentious bastard.

"I am a simple space traveller named Flooge," you psychically transmit, hurriedly adding, "O Mighty One," A bit of fluffy deference usually goes a long way with these timeless celestial bores.

"TRESPASSER FLOOGE, YOU HAVE OFFENDED THIS SANCTIFIED DOMAIN AND MUST FACE MY CHALLENGE!"

Oh, for fucks sake, it's a game player, easily the most annoying type of Deity. Still, you've got no choice but to go along with it, even a half-arsed God like this one can banish you somewhere wildly unpleasant if you upset them.

"I'M IN A BIT OF A HURRY ACTUALLY," booms the voice. "SO I WILL KEEP YOUR CHALLENGE SIMPLE."

You watch two swirling, temporal rifts appear in the rotating crystal-scape as you wonder why an ageless time God that exists beyond the boundaries of Space Time is in 'a hurry'.

"CHOOSE YOUR PATH FLOOGE. ONE WILL LEAD YOU BACK TO WHERE YOU TRESPASSED UPON MY DOMAIN. THE OTHER WILL TRANSPORT YOU TO ANOTHER SEGMENT OF YOUR TIMESCAPE."

Well, that's just great, an arbitrary 50% chance of being slung to a random point in your life by some jumped up, self-important time-wrangler. They usually like to throw in a riddle or something.

"Is there a clue of some sort, O Wondrous Lord of Time? Perhaps you'd like to provide one in the form of a clever riddle?"

"DO NOT TEST MY BENEVOLENCE INFILTRATOR FLOOGE - I'D APPRECIATE IT IF YOU SPEED THIS UP. LIKE I SAY I AM IN A HURRY."

To reinforce the point, the crystal structure begins to rapidly shrink around you. There's no time to appeal further, you need to make a choice…

If you would like to pass through the temporal rift on the left. ***Go to page 44****.*

Or

If you would like to pass through the temporal rift on the right. ***Go to page 38****.*

57

SOME TIME LATER IN A NEARBY STAR SYSTEM

Kevin was almost beyond excitement as he galloped up the hill to meet Penelope, his wild, green mane blowing in the wind and both of his penises rotating anticlockwise.

He had bested all of her other suitors in single knife combat. Clive the Insufferable, Derek the Deliberate and Roger the Enthusiastic all lay in a dead heap behind his uncle's pie shop, ready to be ground down into pie filling.

As he reached the lookout station he saw her, silhouetted by the setting sun, casually carving a poem into a tree with her horn.

He stopped a respectful distance away and brayed the customary mating call:

"Virginal Maiden Penelope. I, Kevin the Practical have slain all other suitors for your hoof. I now respectfully request that you allow me full mating rights for a period of no less that six months."

There was an awkward pause. Penelope sighed and turned to face him. She had clearly been crying, his penises stopped rotating almost immediately.

"Oh, I just don't know Kevin," she blurted and began gently sobbing. "I just always thought that I'd go to College and get my certificate of plough maintenance before I settled down. Everything's just happening so fast, especially since Dad fell into that thresher…"

Kevin trotted over and swooped his mane over her head in a display of nurturing comfort. "But I killed all my friends," he said, "like you asked me to."

"I know," she sobbed. "I'm sorry about that."

"Look," he said, "let's pray together to our glorious Lord Equestron to give us a sign. If he answers then lets forget the formal rutting ceremony and run away together. You can study for your ploughing certificate and I'll do contract killings to pay the rent."

"Oh Kevin, you always were such a dreamer."

"Just pray with me Penelope, pray to Equestron for a sign."

As they chanted and gazed towards the rose tinted evening sky, a bright flash of pink light sparkled across the horizon directly in front of them.

“Equestron speaks! He speaks!” squealed Penelope “It is meant to be! Take me away from all this, Kevin, Take me away!”

“At once my love. As Equestron has decreed so shall it be!” He reared up on his hind legs, triumphantly rotated his penises in different directions and the happy couple galloped together into the sunset.

Kevin and Penelope would never know but the pink flash that they saw was not a sign from their strange god. It was actually the light from the huge explosive destruction of the Pungent Defiler reaching their planet 200 light years after Commander Flooge pulled the wrong string on his tactical manoeuvre hammock and flew straight into an asteroid.

Earth Conquering status: While trying to transport the remnants of the earth to a refinery, you decided that you would be better at flying a spaceship than a computer. Your subsequent fiery death inadvertently inspired the development of a massively dysfunctional relationship that would leave hundreds dead and a respected pie chain out of business.

Galactic Consolidated Rank: Conqueror, level 3 (obliterated via misadventure).

The End.

59

MEANWHILE ON A PLANET IN A COMPLETELY DIFFERENT DIMENSION

Shania was really at the end of her tether. For the third night this week, the twins from the next cave over, Yasmine and Simon, had just stormed in, stolen all of the firewood she had gathered today and eaten her few scraps of food. Then they smashed the place up a bit, beat her soundly and finally, in what she assumed was a gesture of dominance and intimidation, shat on the floor, one after the other, maintaining unblinking eye contact with her throughout.

She could live with the thievery and violence, but even for a squalid community of primitive cave dwellers, the floor shitting thing was just unnecessary.

She'd just finished cleaning the place up and was tucking into the scrap of cat meat that she had successfully hidden in a small rock pile when she suddenly noticed a metal box with flashing lights had appeared in the middle of her cave.

Somehow managing to not choke on a particularly stringy bit of cat leg, Shania cowered away from this flashing intruder, eyes wide and fearful. A noise emerged from the machine:

"Sentience de-fragmentation loop complete. Commander? Commander Flooge?"

Shania had no idea what the strange noises were, but they sounded friendly enough. She performed the introductory grunts that her tribe used for semi-formal events and held up a half chewed bit of cat as an offering for the metal box.

"Hmmm, looks like a dimension shift," mused the computer "Is that fried feline? Thanks, but no thanks."

Shania was confused, she grunted and hummed a phrase that would translate roughly as "suit yourself" and settled back onto her haunches to finish off her meal.

A golden ray of light shone out from the computer into Shania's left eye and in an instant the language and reasoning portions of her brain were mutated forward a few hundred generations.

"Can you understand me now?" asked the computer.

“Y.. y.. yes,” replied Shania, surprised and amazed at the language she was suddenly able to comprehend and speak.

“Right,” chirped the computer, “that’s a start. Now, did you know that those pig bones you’ve got piled up in the corner make excellent tools or weapons?”

“Wea-pons?” asked Shania, staring at the dark metal rectangle, eyes wide. As the concept began to take hold in what passed for her temporal lobe, she sorted through the pile for the heaviest, sharpest bone she could find. Hefting the ideal candidate in her hand, Shania headed out of the cave on a mission of fecal retribution that was the first messy step on her species’ epic journey to the stars...

Back onboard the Pungent Defiler, you stare at the gap on the command deck where the computer used to be. Wondering why the ‘Help’ button was greyed out, I mean what was the point of it even being there? Moments later the ship self-destructs, vapourizing you into an angry, confused, fine mist.

Earth Conquering Status: You destroyed the earth in order to turn a quick profit and then died in an unrelated password related disaster. Your computer went on to become the ruler/ deity of a race that eventually destroyed all biological life in a parallel universe. You always knew there was something wrong with it.

Galactic Consolidated Rank: Conqueror Level 3, missing presumed exploded.

The End.

61

THE SUNK COST FAIL-ACY

"Excellent news, Commander Flooge," beams the horrific Earth visage of the UN Secretary General from the holo-screen.

"Are you going to finally pass the fucking resolution today?" You ask for what seems like the hundredth time.

"Absolutely, yes."

You perk up, "Really? It's going to happen?"

"Yes, the resolution recognising the 3rd stage of the funding bid for the investigative panel is going to the floor today. We're really pulling out all the stops, procedurally speaking."

You deflate, both figuratively and literally.

The secretary general continues "It should be a straight run through the panel towards a full floor vote on the surrender motion in no time at all."

Turning off the screen you retreat to the holo-lounge to enjoy a few more episodes of *'Black Hole Transit Guards: Uncut'*. You know you really should just laser the whole UN building and get on with putting the Earth's population in work camps - but you've spent nearly half a Cycle waiting, why not give them a little longer?

The answer to that question arrives in the form of a swarm of virus missiles that the Earth creatures must have been developing during the time that the UN have been expertly tying you up in red tape.

The computer and the automated defences manage to take out most of the missile swarm, but a couple get through, puncture the hull and release a nasty pathogen into the ship.

You're far too wrapped up in an especially outrageous bit of Transit Guard behaviour to pay any attention to the computer setting off a number of warning alarms.

You notice a slight itch near your scent bladder, shiver slightly and then swell up and explode all over the inside of the holo-lounge.

Earth Conquering Status: You were fatally outwitted by a group of career bureaucrats - it's just as well you were horribly

exploded by a weaponised virus as you'd never live this down back at the office. The Earth remains unconquered.

Galactic Consolidated Rank: You were so overdue in reporting back on the fate of your mission that you were due to be demoted to Junior Admin Assistant level 2 on your return. So a laser bolt dodged there, in a way.

The End.

63

AN INCREDIBLY MARGINAL PROMOTION

You extend yourself to your full height, semi-dilate your pleasure cavity to denote formal annoyance and modulate your psychic communication to maximum self-righteousness.

"I'll thank you to stay your countdown, Auditor, for I, Commander Flooge of the Pungent Defiler have purged our galaxy of a vile, racist civilisation - one that should not have been tolerated upon even the most basic of three dimensional platforms. Behold."

With a gestural flourish you transmit the evidence of Earth's horrendous bigotry to the Audit craft. The auditor's brain stalks quiver slightly while they process the offending material.

"Right, ok. I see… Oh hold on. Yes, that's actually quite bad isn't it?"

"Indeed."

"The Audit process is suspended, Commander Flooge. While we cannot condone the waste of potential planetary resources through your use of the CrashLoop protocol, you were mildly justified in the outright obliteration of an aberrant civilisation. As such we recommend that your rank is promoted by point zero zero one."

With that, the Auditor vanishes from your deck and the hulking Audit Craft slides into a new dimensional rift, off to make some other poor bastard's life miserable, no doubt. When you are sure they are gone, you relax and your tension bladder deflates with relief, all over the floor.

You stand in a sulphurous pool of your own making, staring at the empty space where the Earth used to be. Not for the first time, you wonder if it is too late to re-train as a teacher.

"Congratulations on your big promotion, Commander," chirps the computer.

Earth Conquering Status: You justifiably obliterated the Earth and its entire civilization because of their offensive, anti-tentacular bigotry.

Galactic Consolidated Rank: Conqueror, level 2.999.

The End.

64

A CLONE DOME HOME OF YOUR OWN

For what seems the first time in ages, something goes your way. On aborting the sentience de-frag the computer comes straight back on line and ceases the self-destruct countdown.

“Well, someone got themselves in a bit of a mess didn’t they?”

“Whatever, just bring all systems back online.”

“And I mean that figuratively and literally,” it continues, letting loose all the cleaning drones to tidy up the messy state that you have let the command deck become.

“I’m warning you,” you snap “I’ll... I’ll...“

“What turn me off again and nearly blow yourself up? Be my guest, I’m backed up at GCHQ.”

“Whatever,” you mumble. “Just pilot us to the refinery. I’m going for a long steam cleanse.”

“Take your time.” it chirps as you slither off to the hygienarium, you feel a mild rumble as the thrusters fire up and the ship heads into the nebula.

Two-thirds of a DemiCycle later and you arrive at the refinery, offload your cargo and abandon all plans to make a return trip. You give the refinery the coordinates for the remains of the Earth and hand over salvage rights, you’ll probably only get a fraction of what you could have earned, but the payment from this load alone will be more than you’ve ever earned in one mission.

Using the mobile dimension rift that is tethered to the refinery you jump to a clone facility you’ve had your eye on for a while, pick out an especially functional looking dome and authorise payment.

You transport-beam to the dome, squat over the grow-pool and, with a small splash, excrete a shiny dna pellet into the pale liquid.

You’re not one for sentimentality, but the sight of the brown lump slowly staining the bottom of the grow pool makes all of your hearts skip a beat.

Two Cycles later - as the Pungent Defiler is sinking inexorably into a lake of acidic, star-beast vomit, you use the very last bit of power to call up a live feed of your clone dome. The last thing your eyeball sees before it pops and melts is a tiny tentacle unfurling from inside the grow pool.

You expire with that corny line from an old holo-play running through your minds...

"Violently aggressive commercial practices and viral dna stimulation under radioactive bombardment... finds a way."

Earth conquering status: You destroyed a whole planetary civilisation so that you could make a copy of yourself, which was just as well as you went on to be melted by a huge, extra-dimensional monster that was suffering from food poisoning.

Galactic Consolidated Rank: Conqueror, level 2.8 (at time of death).

The End

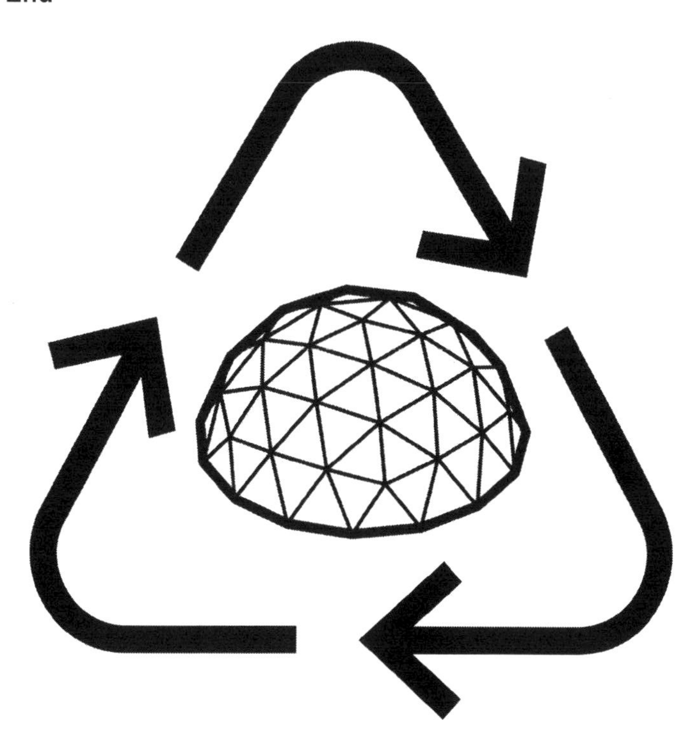

AN AD-HOC APPRAISAL - ROUND 2

As you are sucked through the Exit Y tunnel you are suddenly certain that you made the wrong choice, therefore you are delighted that rather than being flung into the slow death of the de-constitution pit, you exit into a new white cube room.

"Appraisal Round 2." Announces a different, slightly gruff, voice as the tunnel portal slides shut behind you.

"Ensure your olfactory senses are attuned to maximum sensitivity and evaluate the two scents emerging from these exits"

An exit opens on the left side wall, you direct your senses towards it, the savory smell of fried dark-matter nuggets wafts from the portal. A second exit opens on the right side wall, you direct your sensory glands towards it. A vile stench that appears to be made up of the concentrated waste products of some diseased lifeform hits your olfactory senses so hard that one of your hearts stops briefly. You wipe a tear way from your eye as the gruff voice rings out.

"Choose the exit that you feel most reflects your personal ethics. You have one MicroCycle to exit before mandatory de-constitution."

If you want to go through the wholesome, welcoming food smell exit. ***Go to page 46****.*

Or

If you want to make it clear that your ethical approach is akin to that of the smell of a diseased death sewer, take that exit. ***Go to page 82****.*

WHO COULD HAVE PREDICTED THAT THERE IS NO HONOUR AMONGST THIEVES?

It's been a while since you had to do a system lookup manually, but there is something strangely satisfying about flipping switches and manipulating the tacto-pad to scroll through holographic maps to find somewhere suitably commercial, but well outside of Galactic Consolidated control.

You eventually settle on an anarchist trading system just outside the realm of the Yorg (a tiresome, sponge-based, hive mind that spans a thousand systems or and seems to have no aims other than to be as bouncy as possible), well away from any GC infrastructure.

It's only a couple of hyper jumps so you decide to programme the route and retire to the holo-lounge for the duration of the trip. You're nervous about using the transport tank without a fully functional and less annoying computer, plus you've got series five of *'The Ongoing Actual Disputes Of a Dark Matter Extractor Clone Family'* to watch - and the end of series four was a real cliff hanger, both gravitationally and emotionally speaking.

After an intensely relaxing OptiCycle or so, a small pinging alarm from the command console notifies you that you are approaching your destination.

Takplott V is a grey, cloudy, swirling planet which is home to millions of trading posts. Only a few are willing to deal with volatile resources like TCP, so you choose the first on the list and set a sub-orbital course.

The trading post is a series of opaque domes that look like they might have been carved out of rock, they sit in the middle of a wild grassy plain. In fact most of the surface of the planet is wild grassy plain, which is constantly being set alight by the landing jets and launch thrusters of all the trade traffic. At any time about a quarter of the planet is on fire, which explains the swirling, cloudy skies and why everyone who lives here has a cough.

You've arranged to meet a potential buyer in Dome 8, they go by the obvious alias 'Affected Mallone' and claim to be part of the legendary 'Haze Tribute' smuggling syndicate. If that's true then, they'll definitely have the funds and the means to take all the TCP off your tentacles.

68

You manage to find a spot right next to Dome 8 to land, once the flames have died down to a manageable level, you lower the ramp and slither across the smouldering landscape - you might be new to the black-market life, but you're not naive enough to trust any local transport beams on a burning crime planet.

The interior of Dome 8 is essentially a chaotic trade bazaar and stimulant den set up around a central enquiry desk. Beings of all shapes, sizes and temporal status crowd the place, transacting all manner of illegal and unhygienic business.

You approach the desk and a fleshy red sphere rises up to meet you.

"Please provide me with your enquiry, fellow criminal." it transmits breezily into your main brain.

"I am here to meet Affected Mallone, where are they located?" You think back.

"One moment while I check our manifests, my crooked colleague."

The sphere flashes for a moment or two, then continues.

"You can find Affected Mallone in the lounge area just behind you, he's the tri-ped cyborg with six glass arms." It descends back behind the desk with a gurgling sound.

You slither into the lounge, it is virtually deserted except for a couple of cloud lizards playing cards and a ridiculously shiny cyborg sitting in the corner trying to look inconspicuous. It isn't easy to go unnoticed when most of you is made of polished chrome and a majority of your limbs are refracting any available light into bright rainbows all over the walls.

You slither up to the table and rest your self on the bench across from the smuggler.

"You Flooge?" The cyborg transmits.

"Yes," you respond, "and you're Affected Mallone?"

"I may be."

"I was led to believe that you have the means to purchase a shipload of TCP - with incurring any.... Galactic Consolidated entanglements."

"Well that's the real trick isn't it?" Mallone sighs flatly. "That your ship just there?" It gestures towards the Pungent Defiler through a nearby viewport.

"Yes." You reply.

A sudden burst of laser fire erupts from under the table leaving half of you a smouldering lump of flesh and the rest of you slowly dying and thoroughly paralysed.

"Let me give you some advice," Affected Mallone offers. "Always shoot first and ask questions later."

"But.. but..." You whimper, telepathically, 'you asked me at least three questions before you shot me."

"Well, if you're so fucking clever then why are you shot to bits on the floor and I'm about to make off with your ship and your cargo?"

You can barely summon the energy to form words but you just about manage: "That's another question."

Enraged, Affected Mallone, raises a shiny leg and stomps the remaining life out of you.

"How do you like that?" The shiny cyborg screams at the puddle that was you just a few moments ago. It realises that was a question too and storms off to plunder your ship and re-think its whole rhetorical game.

Earth Conquering Status: You mined the smouldering remains of the earth and tried to become a black-market privateer. You were the victim of a highly predictable, pre-emptive murder by a shiny smuggler with a subconscious enquiry problem.

Galactic Consolidated rank: Fugitive, level 5.

The End.

70

UNTIL THE NEXT CENTICYCLE, I JUST KEEP MOVING ON

It's best not to get too attached. As the twelve-time GC Conqueror of the Cycle, Dashkillion Prime, always says: "Conquer 'em mean. Strip 'em clean."

You leave the hooded conspiracists to it and head off for a new mission in the Sirenia Nebula.

Although it takes far longer than you would like, over the next few Cycles, the Brotherhood of Enlightenment gradually increase the revenue from their achingly slow domination of the Earth.

Finally - just as you have finished putting down a minor rebellion in a star system populated by floating jelly monsters - you get a ping from accounts that the Earth account is now fully operational.

You steam cleanse some stubborn remnants of semi-sentient, floating jelly off yourself and check with the computer for your next assignment. You've been on a real roll lately, not wasting anymore time on conquering Earth was one of the best decisions you've ever made.

You laser a couple of jelly cities into oblivion before you head off, just to celebrate how well things are going.

Earth Conquering Status: You left a slow, but determined, secret world government to conquer the world on your behalf. They eventually managed it and with the time you saved, you really got your career moving in the right direction.

Galactic Consolidated Rank: Conqueror, level 2.3.

The End.

71

TWO GC EMPLOYEES ENTER, ONE GC EMPLOYEE LEAVES

"Welcome, Commander Flooge!" The door announces as you slither into the IT workspace, "Conqueror Level three and Massive Sexual Failure."

The pale gang of IT technicians stop whatever work they probably weren't doing anyway to turn and laugh at you. Laughing hardest in the middle of the workspace is the rather athletic - and though you hate to admit it - very good-looking, Klurge.

"Laugh no more, Klurge, I challenge you to Corporately Approved death battle, here and now." You pull a blue tinged laser knife from your weapon pouch, slowly ignite it and point it directly towards the, frankly smouldering, IT head technician. "And yes, before you ask, I have filled in all the forms for this."

"Whoa, calm down, Flooge, We were just having a little joke."

"The time for calm is over you disgusting coward. Your ineptitude and rank lack of professionalism has endangered and insulted me for the last time. I demand satisfaction". You spin your laser knife twice and adopt a 'preparation for dismemberment' combat stance.

"Ok, ok, fair enough," says Klurge, clearly intimidated by your magnificent dominance, they quiver their tentacles in a pattern of reasonableness. "We'll get your computer's sentience back within reasonable parameters and, to make things right, we'll add in some new prescience modules. You'd be the only level three in the whole fleet with a prescient AI. How's that?"

You relax slightly and lower your laser knife. You'd still really like to kill Klurge, but a new prescient AI could really get your career on the fast track.

"And of course - I'll restore your company profile description to something far more appropriate."

"Good, yes, get on with it," you thunder, trying not to sound too pleased. This is going so well, you really must start challenging more colleagues to laser knife death battles from now on.

"Right, what would be most respectful and appropriate?" muses Klurge lifting something from beneath his desk. "How about...", they hiss, igniting the red laser knife now clutched in a dominant tentacle, "Deceased?"

Klurge leaps over the desk to land a short distance in front of you, and flips the laser knife from tentacle to tentacle while adopting a worryingly experienced-looking 'circle of doom' combat stance.

"No one fucks with the IT Department," snarls Klurge before emitting a semi-gaseous spurt of challenge fluid and charging towards you.

The battle is joined!

If you want to best Klurge with your no-doubt superior laser-knife skills and win the fear and respect of the IT department via a spectacular and needlessly vicious workplace murder. ***Go to page 77****.*

Or

If you want to ensure victory by using the password secretly conditioned into all IT staff that will cause Klurge to experience a brief momentary full body muscle spasm, allowing you to administer an unblockable death stab. ***Go to page 89****.*

73

EIGHT THOUSAND NOT AT ALL EASY INSTALMENTS

"Do not concern yourself, puny Countmaster," you bluster "I shall merely realise some minor assets and holdings and forward the amount you required within the next DemiCycle."

"If I may be permitted to know, mighty Flooge, which assets exactly are you referring to?"

"How dare you! You pitiful spreadsheet wrangler. My private finances are none of your concern." You are definitely in a lot of trouble now.

"I'm afraid in this situation, they very much are. Our tabulation scan of your assets reveals only a credit account containing zero point Seven Quantics, an extensive collection of 'Non-simulated Matri-Clones of Glaarp' holo tapes and two Maskillion Creepstalker corpses. So, all together your assets total zero point eight Quantics. Which I am sure that someone as clever and impressive as you will appreciate is significantly less than twenty-four Quantics."

This is a fucking nightmare, you need to get out of here quick. Time to ping the ship and get it to transport you out of here.

"You see this switch here?" Drex asks you as it flips a small, orange toggle on the wall "It disables all communication and transport beams from operating in this room."

Drex pulls a small plasma blaster from within it's messy tangle of tentacles and levels it at you. "While this is just a precaution for my own safety."

"This is an outrage," you attempt to bluster, but are struggling to not sound concerned, "I can... perhaps pay in instalments?"

"An option I have already considered, most thoughtful Flooge. But as your basic cyclical salary is eight Quantics and the cumulative cyclical interest rate on such a debt is twelve thousand percent - I'm afraid such a plan will not be feasible."

"So, I suppose the only option is... is... " you almost blub

"Yes," confirms Drex, "a compulsory ad-hoc appraisal with the HR department."

You shudder, compulsory ad hoc appraisals are even more

dangerous than the normal ones.

"However..." Muses Drex. The shrivelled accountant glides their hover cushion in your direction, coming to rest uncomfortably nearby. You don't know where this is going, but you are sure it isn't good.

"I could perhaps pull a few strings with a clone batch mate of mine in the sanitation department" One of their tentacles flops loose and brushes against the side of your dorsal mass.

"Maybe you could work off your debt there? If you wanted me to help you?" The tentacle caresses your anterior nerve mass as Drex maintains deeply uncomfortable eye contact and keeps the plasma blaster levelled at you.

"If you were my special friend, you could probably pay that nasty debt off in, say, eight thousand CentiCycles." Drex slowly circles your frontal pleasure cavity with a couple of tentacles, before attempting an exploratory insertion. "You want to be my special friend don't you Flooge?" Moans the accountant.

If you want to be Drex's 'special friend'. ***Go to page 99****.*

Or

If you'd rather try your luck with an ad-hoc HR Appraisal instead of being repeatedly violated by a creepy accountant while working in a sewer. ***Go to page 75****.*

75

AN AD-HOC APPRAISAL - ROUND 1

You find yourself at the entry gangway for the Appraisal Process, you and a range of other appraisees are dotted about on a series of converging travelator lanes heading toward the embarkation point.

As you slide forwards, a series of messages are played in your main brain.

"Welcome Galactic Consolidated Staff Member to the Appraisal Process. Please note that you have now passed the point of no return and may not exit the process unless you wish to volunteer for pre-emptive de-constitution.

The results of the process are entirely binding in accordance with the terms of your GC employment contract and will be executed by HR advisors where necessary.

If you do not have a current set of post-death instructions and would like to establish them before you enter the process, please visit the station on the right of the embarkment point."

You are nearly at the end of the travelator, and see almost the whole Appraisal Process stretching out before you, it hasn't changed much from the last time you had to do it, but the smell is definitely worse. An interconnected maze of rooms and tunnels is suspended over a vast de-constitution pit, where unsuccessful appraisees are constantly being melted down to make material for new clone moulds (and industrial lubricants). The smell of the pit and the screams that emerge from it are often used in GC motivational materials.

The travelator deposits you at the embarkation point through a blue forcefield that disables all of your remote communication and transport capabilities as well as scanning for any non-permitted support upgrades.

Four lanes over from you an appraisee is having a Logic Booster noisily hacked out of them by an HR Advisor.

"When you are ready to begin please use the entrance marked with your name and rank."

As you wait to be assigned an entrance, you are distracted by the arrhythmic splatter of appraisees being expelled from the process at various points and dropped into the de-constitution pit.

"Flooge, Conqueror Level Three, embark at entrance B immediately."

You slither over to transparent tube in question and after a brief pause are sucked through the tube into a small, blank white room to begin the process. To say that you are nervous would be a colossal understatement, the only thing stopping you spraying the room with fear bile is how low your bodily fluids have become after recent events.

"Appraisal round one," rings out a deceptively friendly voice.

"Please consider the following scenario and then choose the exit that you consider correct..."

Two circular tunnel portals open up in the wall facing you, labelled 'X' and 'Y'.

"Drooge and Twaarj are Level One engineers that work together on a thruster assembly line in a GC mega-factory. They are the closest of friends and have shared many agreeable workplace achievements and sexual encounters together. During a normal shift, Twaarj notices that Drooge's hygienarium break was three NanoCycles longer than company policy allows for.

Should Twaarj take decisive and harsh action against Drooge and report them immediately for this breach with a recommendation for lethal dismemberment (CHOOSE X)

or

Should Twaarj show compassion and understanding towards Drooge and report them immediately for this breach with a recommendation for lethal injection (CHOOSE Y)

You have one MIcroCycle to choose an exit before mandatory de-constitution."

If you want to choose the harsh (but fair) route of EXIT X. ***Go to page 78.***

Or

If you want to choose the soppy, merciful route of EXIT Y. ***Go to page 66.***

77

YOU'VE NEVER BEEN SO EMBARRASSED

As Klurge charges towards you, you speed up your time perception to evaluate your tactics.

While Klurge has a height and mass advantage over you, your extreme cunning and tactical nous is sure to win the day. From the angle of attack, a simple sidestep, slash parry and counter attack should leave Klurge in trouble.

Klurge leaps into a wild over tentacled hack attack, just as you knew they would. You dodge to the left and raise your laser blade to deflect the crude hack. All too easy.

As you hold your blade aloft, a sudden explosive pain rips through your right side. Klurge has shifted their blade to one of their left sided tentacles mid-attack and rammed it into you, hitting a couple of vital organs, several less vital ones and a bundle of quite important nerve clusters.

You stand, completely paralysed, frozen in an awkward pose of extreme pain. Klurge rips the laser knife from your side with a cruel twist and a whole bunch of green gore slops out of the wound and splatters onto the floor of the IT office.

"I was a bit of a pan-district knife murder champ when I was younger," sneers Klurge as they plunge their blade into another equally painful and no doubt vital part of your anatomy.

You die, standing there. Bled to death at the hands of a lowly but handsome IT technician. The totality of your humiliation only matched by the depth of your shame.

A humiliating death is not enough for the IT department though, they nail your corpse to the wall and use your pleasure cavity as ad-hoc cable storage.

Earth Conquering Status: After destroying the pitiful planet Earth and all of its inhabitants you were horribly murdered in a duel caused by passive aggressive office tension.

Galactic Consolidated Rank: Furniture.

The End

AN AD-HOC APPRAISAL - ROUND 2

You whoosh through the exit X tunnel and land in a new white cube room and the tunnel portal closes behind you.

“Appraisal round 2,” announces the friendly voice.

“Please regard the two dimensional symbols beside the exit portals…”

Two new exit portals open up, on opposite sides of the room. Next to one of them is a purple square surrounded at random intervals by hundreds of small silver stars. The image on the other side of the room is a large eye staring out from a pyramid shape.

“Choose the exit with the symbol that most closely represents where you see your career in five Cycles. You have one MicroCycle to exit before mandatory de-constitution.”

If you want to choose the pretty, but somewhat random square and stars exit. ***Go to page 31****.*

Or

If you want to choose the intriguing, but really rather weird eye in the pyramid exit. ***Go to page 118****.*

79

THE WEST WING

On balance, you think the computer is probably right, taking over as the most powerful politician on the planet is likely the easiest way to get the Earth and it's bizarre inhabitants under your control.

"Ok, let's go with the top down option."

"Excellent decision Commander, shall I commence the transferomatic sequence?"

"I suppose so, no point in delaying things," you sigh.

A panel in the ceiling of the command deck opens up and two container pods descend.

"Transfer sequence initiated, Commander."

The left hand pod fizzes with the purple hue of a transport beam and the vile form of the human 'Myra Eagleton' materialises. It makes some high pitched screaming noises, before the mind probe kicks in and it is subdued.

"Brain patterns read, bodily dimensions copied and locked." States the computer. "You can begin transformatication at your convenience."

You groan and slither into the right hand pod, you really hate this bit. After the pod seals there are few clicks and beeps before a radioactive wave laser de-constitutes your physical matter and re-aligns it in the form of the 'Myra Eagleton'. For a brief moment you twitch and spasm horribly, unable to work out how to control your new and unusual body. Then the computer remembers to apply the vital bits of the brain patterns and you instinctively become able to control the human biology.

"Well, this is humiliatingly limiting," you think as you perceive the ship's deck through the primitive human's senses, "They don't even have x-ray vision."

"I'm afraid there just isn't enough room in the human form to fit in both major and minor telepathic glands, commander."

"Meaning?"

"I won't be able to communicate directly with you on the planet surface without additional equipment."

"Well, that's massively re-assuring - what additional equipment exactly?"

"The device encircling the end of your left upper limb is a time measuring device known as a 'watch' - I've embedded the communicator in there, it will act as a psychic relay."

"OK, that actually seems sensible, but if you lose contact at all, you need to immediately transport me back from my last known location."

"Of course, commander. As long as you have the watch I'll be linked constantly to your coordinates, you have nothing to worry about."

You have serious doubts that this is the case. Still, how badly wrong can things go? You're a hyper-intelligent, planet-conquering sophisticate of the galaxy and the Earthlings have probably only just stopped living in caves. This really should be very easy.

"Fine, upload language and localisation info and commence transport. I don't want to spend any more time like this than I have to."

There's a fuzzy feeling in what you suddenly know to call your 'head' as the computer dumps the localisation settings into one of the few sub-brains that this measly body can hold. The purple haze of the transport beam kicks in and the deck of the Pungent Defiler blurs away and you materialize sitting in a circular shaped room that your sub-brain informs you is known as the 'Oval Office'.

You're just marvelling at what a total dump this is, when a psychic transmission from the computer is relayed via the watch:

"Checking status, Commander. Is everything optimal?"

"Yes," you think back, "I'm ready to begin".

"Very well, Commander. Standing by."

After a quick sub-brain scan to determine the purpose of the laughably primitive communications equipment on your desk, you press the intercom button.

"Yes, Madam President?" Asks a voice.

81

If you want to summon your military leaders, in order to start some sort of global conflict to divide and rule the human civilisation. ***Go to page 129***.

Or

If you want to pursue a strategy of global disarmament to weaken the planet's defences as far as possible to make it super easy to conquer later on. ***Go to page 131***.

AN AD-HOC APPRAISAL - ROUND 3

You whizz through a transparent tunnel tube and emerge into yet another white cube room, the portal to the tunnel slides closed and you wait for the next round to begin.

Without any announcement, two new exits open up in the wall you are facing.

Nothing happens.

You wait.

Still nothing happens.

You would have thought that a pause from extremely tense career or death decisions would calm you down but the silence and uncertainty is playing absolute havoc with the waste expulsion end of your anatomy. The nearest hygienarium is going to take some serious punishment if you can get through this alive and fully constituted.

A voice suddenly booms into your head, “Choose.”

Choose what? Choose an exit? What are the options?

“Choose.” Yells the voice again unhelpfully, “Choose.”

To underscore this instruction the floor begins to slowly slide open from behind you, revealing the horror of the de-constitution pit below.

“Choose.” bellows the voice, the floor is sliding faster now, you are going to have to make a random choice and trust your luck, which based on recent events is not in fantastic shape.

“Choose.” Screams the voice.

If you want to decisively jump into the left exit. ***Go to page 53****.*

Or

If you'd like to prevaricate until the very last second when you are about to you run out of floor, paralysed by uncertainty and unable to decide, while the voice screams the word “Choose” at you a couple more times before finally scrambing into the right exit. ***Go to page 43****.*

83

GRATUITOUS AND COSTLY ACTION SET PIECE

You notice Countmaster Drex begin to drift towards a small panel of switches on the wall - one of them might be a transport blocker - you telepathically ping the computer to transport you now. Nothing happens.

You throw yourself across the room, just as the accountant is reaching for an orange switch on the panel, you collide heavily and Drex's tentacle is pulled away from flicking the switch at the very last moment.

You knock Drex from their hover pillow and both of you land on the floor in a mess of tentacles and rage bile. You ping the computer to transport you again, but still nothing happens.

Drex hops up and makes a break towards the switch panel, you grab a trailing tentacle and easily haul them back towards you, your tentacles primed to perform a Mandraxian death hug.

Before you can envelop your foe, Drex quickly spins and produces a small plasma blaster from somewhere, firing two rapid blasts. The first incinerates the motivational laser-squid poster and the second singes a sucker on one of your dorsal tentacles.

Ignoring the pain, you quickly close the gap between you and the accountant and make a grab for the blaster. You converge in a mass of writhing tentacles, wrestling to get control of the weapon, plasma blasts ping around the room, but somehow you are not hit.

Finally you are able to get some leverage and manage to slowly rotate the blaster until it is shakily pointing at Drex's straining body. At the very moment you tense your muscles to pull the trigger, you feel an itchy tingle and find yourself transported to the deck of the Pungent Defiler.

"Apologies for the transporter delay, Commander, I was on another call."

You don't have time to discuss how that doesn't make any sense at all.

"Just get us out of here - fast", you snap. "And plot a hyperjump to the nearest non-GC system as soon as we are at minimum safe distance from the dock."

"Affirmative, thrusting now."

You brace yourself for a rapid departure, but instead the computer sedately reverses you from the docking bay and slowly spins the ship towards the exit. One holoscreen flashes up a tactical display showing two GC security drones closing in fast.

"What the fuck are you doing? We need to get out of here now!"

"Apologies commander, but I have to conform to docking bay safety protocols at all -"

"Switch to manual control now."

"I'm not sure that is a very good-"

A laser blast from one of the security drones flashes across the viewscreen. Drones don't tend to miss a sitting target, so that was probably a warning shot, which means they want to take you alive, which is bad. Very, very bad.

You slap the manual override switch on the command console and switch into 'Urgent Flee' mode, your tactical manoeuvre hammock drops down and you jump in, immediately gunning the thrusters and executing an evasive spiral thrust towards the docking bay doors.

More laser fire from the drones bursts around you, a couple of shots pepper the rear of the Pungent Defiler. You feel relieved that at least now they are trying to kill you a bit.

With a deft tug on the offensive strings of your hammock you fire back at the drones, one explodes dramatically, the other is hit by debris from the explosion, it loses control and plows into a slow moving freighter just leaving its berth. The shockwave from the resulting explosion rattles your primary endoskeleton.

"Ha Haaaaa!", you exclaim. You are now a third of the way to the docking bay entrance and the drones are off your tail.

"That freighter was carrying three thousand juvenile clones on an educational visit," intones the computer, "just so you know".

You ignore it and engage full afterburner thrust, you are now halfway to the docking bay entrance, a few outraged private ships are taking potshots at you but, nothing that your masterful evasive skills can't cope with.

With a slight jerk, the colossal doors of the docking bay begin to close. You should easily be able to make it through in time, but you dial back the stylishness of your evasive maneuvers to make sure.

A tactical alarm rings out to let you know that two AI-missiles are rapidly converging with yourship, there's no way to evade them, but you deploy psychic wave counter-measures to confuse their tracking systems and hope you can make it through the door and hyperjump before they reach you.

"Sensors indicate a grab beam is being charged," moans the computer, "somewhere near the docking bay exit."

You scan the traffic between you and the exit, sure enough a security cruiser has moved into position just in front of the now half closed doors.

"Give it up, Flooge," rings out an angry voice over the external comms channel, "Power down now and we'll give you a reasonably quick death. If you make us use the grab beam, you know we'll have to hand you over to HR..."

"I don't think so," you reply, blocking external comms and loading a firing solution into your gravitational magnetotron.

The deep blue light of a grab beam shines out from the security cruiser and surrounds the Pungent Defiler. Your forward momentum rapidly diminishes as the docking bay doors slide closer together.

You wait until you are exactly midway between the closing AI missiles and the security cruiser, and then fire the magnetotron. A magno gravitational wave deflects the AI missiles in a circular path around your stricken ship and straight into the cruiser, blowing it to pieces.

Freed from the grab beam, you triumphantly gun the thrusters towards the now very nearly closed docking bay doors.

"This is going to be close," you think as the Pungent Defiler shoots through the barely big enough gap and into open space.

"Hyper-jump now!" You scream at the computer.

Nothing happens.

86

“Hyper-jump now!” you scream again.

Absolutely nothing happens. You pull wildly at the strings of the control hammock, it has no effect. Lights blink and fade as the ship powers down and drifts in space. Someone or something has remotely switched off the Pungent Defiler.

A huge, fearsome silver battlecraft pulls in front of you and locks you in a grab beam.

“Flooge, Conqueror level 3 and Fugitive level five. You are now subject to Galactic Consolidated terminal disciplinary procedures. Prepare for transport to the nearest HR department.”

The tingle of the transporter beam is the last sensation you ever feel that isn’t pain.

Earth Conquering Status: After running up an unpayable debt while blowing up the earth, you then engaged in a dramatic, exciting, but ultimately pointless attempt to avoid a dire fate - which you were ultimately subjected to by a vengeful HR department. The whole thing seems like it should be some sort of metaphor, but you don’t know what for.

Galactic Consolidated Rank: Despised Fugitive, level 5 (soon to be deceased).

The End.

87

DEMOTED WITH EXTREME PREJUDICE

You emerge from the latest tunnel into a rather drab, grey, circular space you recognise as an adjudication chamber. The appraisal is over and the good news is that you aren't dead.

The friendly sounding voice rings out, "Flooge, Conqueror Level three. Your appraisal responses have been deemed unsatisfactory, but not worthy of termination. Congratulations."

So, you're not getting melted down for parts, but 'unsatisfactory' is still highly worrying - if you leave this chamber with all your bits and pieces fully intact, that will be a result.

"Your role has been re-assigned to Waste Disposal Technician, level one. The service and administration charges relating to this re-assignment have been debited from your accounts and as such you are required to perform continuous service for 50 Cycles to repay this debt."

A new exit opens in the grey wall of the chamber, a hot waft of what is unmistakably sewage assaults your senses, so you turn them down to bare minimum.

"Please pass through this exit to begin your new assignment. Flooge, Waste Disposal Technician, level one"

Another hole opens up in the floor of the chamber, the even worse smell of the de-constitution pit rises from it, you turn a cluster of your senses off all together.

"Alternatively, in recognition of your Cycles of moderately useful service, you may also voluntarily de-constitute if you deem that preferable to your new assignment."

So, a probable lifetime of working as a slave in the GC sewage department, or an agonizing slow melting death. It's a genuinely tough decision. You suppose there's always some hope that there might be some route out of a lifetime of excrement management, so you should probably submit yourself to the demotion and see what comes of it.

As you slither, resigned to your dirty, smelly fate, towards the waste management exit, a new thunderous voice booms into your consciousness.

“PITIFUL BEING! HALT YOUR COURSE!”

You stop. What the fuck was that?

“I AM CHRONOX, TEMPORAL LORD OF THIS TIME QUADRANT,” the voice yells uncomfortably into your brain.

“YOUR TIMELINE HAS BEEN CORRUPTED AND MUST BE CORRECTED - OUR MEETING MUST OCCUR.”

This is interesting, usually temporal deities are a complete pain in the anterior bilge sac, what with all the time-bending and their penchant for subjecting non-godly life to all manner of games and riddles. You’ve never heard of one trying to correct a timeline before…

“A TEMPORAL RIFT HAS BEEN ESTABLISHED IN THE THREE DIMENSIONAL SPACE BELOW YOUR CURRENT LOCATION, ENTER IT AT ONCE TO RETURN TO THE POINT WHERE THE TIME SCHISM OCCURRED.”

“You want me to jump into the acid death pit hole?” you ask.

“AT ONCE, PUNY FLOOGE CREATURE. PROCEED RAPIDLY. I HAVE LITERALLY A MILLION OTHER THINGS TO DO,” the voice of ‘Chronox’ screams.

If you want to ignore what is almost certainly a hoax by the producers of the popular holo-show 'Amusing Death Conundrums' and submit yourself to a lifetime of quite literally shovelling shit. ***Go to page 102***.

Or

If you want to risk jumping into a pool of acid and slowly dissolving to death because a voice in your head said that it was a God and that it really wanted to meet you. ***Go to page 44***.

MEET THE NEW HEAD OF I.T. SUPPORT SUB-NEST 53/Q

You backflip away from Klurge's initial attack - and it's just as well, they performed a devastating, mid-jump knife shift which you would never have seen coming.

Klurge charges again, you feint to dodge right, but instead at the last second spring upwards to leap over the onrushing IT Team leader.

A searing pain in your dorsal tentacle cluster announces that Klurge anticipated your feint and slashed you as you jumped.

A couple of your minor tentacles slap onto the hard IT department floor, quite some distance from where the rest of you lands.

You are leaking a fairly serious amount of life fluid and you haven't even had the chance to put a scratch on Klurge, this is not how you thought this was going to go.

"This is not how you thought this was going to go, is it?" sneers Klurge, "Didn't you know I was a pan-district knife murder champion in my youth?".

With that the rugged IT technician plunges toward you, ready to administer a horribly fatal attack. You position yourself as though you are going to perform a spinning tentacle sweep, and Klurge hoists his laser knife for a vertical slash drop.

With almost certain death about to strike, you mentally transmit the password phrase "Clean Desk Policy". Klurge suffers an almost imperceptible shudder as all motor functions are shut down for a brief moment. Their eye stares at you in complete surprise just before you plunge your laser blade deep into it.

Klurge lands stone dead right on top of you, the red laser blade skittering harmlessly away and embedding itself in a nearby terminal.

You pull yourself out from under the well toned corpse, covered in a vile and smelly mixture of your own life fluids and some of Klurge's innards.

The staff of the IT sub nest are genuinely stunned.

"I'm genuinely stunned," says one of them.

“Who is going to sign my holiday form now?” Says another.

Extinguishing your laser blade, you slither awkwardly to a nearby wall panel and activate the emergency medical alarm. From a nearby hatch a small drone flies over to you and begins cauterising your severed tentacle wounds. You scream in pain and everyone else flinches as the harsh smell of your cooking flesh fills the office.

A red flashing light and accompanying siren distracts you from the agonizing pain. A large hole opens in the floor and a huge terrifying silver figure emerges. It towers over you, letting out a terrifying roar and expelling a cloud of fear gas as it spins three heavily barbed and dangerous looking limbs around the room, the sharpened claws at the end of each limb snapping noisily in a terrifying display of power and intimidation.

Almost all of the assembled IT staff have emptied their fear sacs all over the floor, which is pretty standard for a visit from the HR department.

“Conqueror Flooge, Level Three”, it roars, “you have committed a workplace murder in accordance with company policy having submitted accurate pre-emptive paperwork. Congratulations.”

That’s a relief, HR are sticklers for process, you heard that Looorg in Section 9 got partially lobotomised after using the wrong form for an office furniture order.

“All assets of the defeated IT Technician Klurge, Team Leader Level two, will now be transferred to your account. Congratulations”

Excellent, Hopefully Klurge had a few Quantics in the bank and you can get some upgrades for the Pungent Defiler.

“You have defeated a superior level colleague and will now assume their duties and responsibilities. Congratulations on your promotion, IT Technician Flooge, Team Leader Level two.”

Hang on - that’s not right, you can’t just become an IT Technician.

“But wait, I’m a -” you begin.

The HR advisor swings all three sharpened clawed limbs to within microns of your most vulnerable bodily parts and lurches its huge and terrifying spiked bulk to tower over you.

91

"Would you like me to refer you to the Frequently Asked Questions board?"

"No. No. No. There's no need for that at all. I am very happy to assume this exciting new role." You gulp in utter terror.

Wordlessly the HR advisor descends back through the floor - the gaping hole seals shut. You consider the gory, slimy, smelly scene before you and ponder just how fate and destiny has led you to this point.

"Can you sign my holiday form?" someone asks.

Earth Conquering Status: You blew up Earth and then murdered your way into an accidental promotion in the IT department. Your immediate future looks like it is going to involve quite a lot of cleaning up.

Galactic Consolidated Rank: IT Technician Team Leader, level 2.

The End.

A ONE-EYED PIRATE

You are standing at the top-of-the-range holo console which is the centrepiece of the shiny, gloss black deck of The PainBrungr - excited by the prospect of the adventurous privateer life that you are about to embark on and relieved at your liberation from the repetitive grind of conquering planets.

"Captain," sighs the rather sensuous voice you chose for the computer, "based on the parameters you supplied, I've selected two alternative targets for our first raid together. Give them a thorough going over and let me know which is your... pleasure."

The imposing viewscreen flashes up a galactimap showing a string of remote desert worlds surrounding a binary star cluster. "This system is run by a crime family of slovenly giant slug monsters, their vast wealth secreted in a series of monster-guarded bunkers, just waiting to be... penetrated."

There is a brief awkward silence, before the sultry tones of the computer continue.

"Alternatively," it moans, "there is a heavily frequented Galactic Consolidated hyper-rift nearby. I've isolated a lightly-guarded convoy of transport barges, swollen with rare minerals, ready to be attacked from behind," it groans, you're starting to think that the whole sexy computer thing was definitely a mistake, "and roughly, thoroughly plundered."

You consider these choices while scrolling through a list of computer voice replacements.

If you want to change your computer's voice interface to 'Wise and old' before heading to the desert planet system to knock off a pile of loot from a slug-led, organised crime network. ***Go to page 113**.*

Or

If you want to change your computer to 'Buoyant' and then intercept the cargo of your former employers. ***Go to page 116**.*

93

GOING NATIVE

Of course you should transport straight back and get on with exploiting an entirely defenceless Earth civilisation. But will you be happy? Will you be cheered wherever you go? Will you get to ask the Pope if you can try his hat on?

"Could you hover over that lake for a minute?" You ask the pilot. As the chopper pauses in the air above one of the great lakes or other, you mentally transmit the supersecret, fifty-two character Meta-Binary passcode that will cause the computer and your ship to spontaneously self-destruct. Then you slide the helicopter door open, remove the watch and toss it into the deep water. "Ok, lets go," you announce.

Seconds later, you notice a brief, small but brilliant flash in the sky, there is no going back now, Flooge is no more. You are free, free from the corporate tyranny of Galactic Consolidated. Free to let Myra Eagleton's personality emerge from your sub-brain and take over your consciousness. Free to be happy. Free to find love. Free to be adored by all the people of the world. Free to go for cocktails with the original cast of Hamilton next Wednesday.

Later, as you are getting ready to go to a celebratory reception in your honour (hosted by Oprah), you see on the news that astronomers are puzzled by a sudden light that appeared in the sky earlier today.

The flash caused by the sudden explosion of the Pungent Defiler will continue to mystify cosmologists and scientists the world over for the rest of human history.

Which is about three weeks.

A GC cleanup crew is dispatched when your ship fails to make a regular quantum ping back to headquarters. Arriving at the manifestly unconquered and now completely undefended planet, they start lasering the place to bits and then round everyone up to be used as slave labour in an especially unpleasant silicon mine on a far flung desert planet.

You are destined to spend your waking hours hacking away at smelly, crystalline rocks with a blunt pickaxe for the rest of your life.

94

Which is about another three weeks.

Earth Conquering Status: With the Earth defenceless and ready to be plundered, you experienced a profound burst of Alternative Personality Override after experiencing genuine happiness for the first time in your life. You did not live happily ever after though.

Galactic Consolidated Rank: Missing, presumed exploded.

The End.

95

MOST ILLUMINATI-ING

“Do a deep political scan,” You instruct the computer, “and you’d better include that moon too. I don’t want another secret moonbase surprise like we had on Gelkron Minor.”

The computer orients a few of the Pungent Defiler’s probe modules at the planet.

“Hmmm,” it mumbles, “that’s interesting.”

“What?”

“Well you were right to be wary of secret surprises, but not on the moon. That’s a total blank. But from monitoring transmissions, it seems like there are three different secret organisations who all seem to be running the planet through proxy governmental methods and primitive societal controls.”

“What sort of controls? Mass hypno-compliance? Could we hack in”

“Noooo - Nothing that advanced. Really basic stuff, subliminal media transcoding, chemicals in transport exhaust fumes, that sort of thing.”

“Well, thats... pitiful. Hang-on - did you say that there are three secret planetary governments?”

“Yes, three of them.”

“Working together or competing?” you ask.

“You’re not going to believe this, but it looks like each of the secret governments are operating completely independently and seemingly unaware of each other’s existence.”

“You’re right. I don’t believe that. How could that even be possible?”

“Pure ineptitude as far as I can tell. You might be less surprised when you learn that one of the secret government is run by a cabal of non-native beings.”

You groan, “Please tell me it’s not shape shifting lizards.”

“It is shape shifting lizards, I’m afraid, quite a gang of them. They seem to have infiltrated the remnants of the Earth civilisation’s feudal hierarchy - so the usual attempt to seize control through largely ceremonial roles and the wearing of crowns."

There's no way you are dealing with some bunch of jumped up reptile subversives again. "What about the other two options?"

"There's a surprisingly advanced - well relatively advanced - group based deep beneath the stretch of water known as the 'Atlantic Ocean', then there's a more loosely dispersed network of affiliated secret societies with a headquarters beneath one of the polar regions."

This is starting to look like far more trouble that a piddling Class 3 civilisation is worth.

If you can't be bothered to deal with any of these seemingly useless secret governments and decide that cowering the earth creatures with a devastating display of power is a better way to go. ***Go to page 37**.*

Or

If you'd rather keep this on the sneaky side and evaluate which of these competing secret rulers of planet Earth to deal with. ***Go to page 121**.*

97

COMMANDER ON DECK

Concentrating hard, you ping out general psychic communications across all the dimensional spectra you have access to, while the computer continues to spout absolute rubbish.

“Huyytoll bass untik groll,” it chunters.

“Lloyding milgrup ssshhhhhh,” it continues.

Suddenly, there is a deep clicking noise and a fuzzy blur across all of your sensory organs as your psychic ping is returned and the computer scans all of your brains.

“Oh, sorry about that, Commander,” it mumbles sheepishly, “I forgot that I had updated your language cortex to local settings already, you may have experienced some linguistic dissonance upon revival, but that should be resolved now.”

Brilliant, you’ve got a computer that forgets things - you’ll string Klurge up by their scent sacs when you get back to HQ. That’s assuming you can make it back across 6th dimensional space with this digital dullard doing the driving.

The suspension fluid drains from the tank, you are blasted with steam to remove the remaining slime and you are able to fully stretch out all of your tentacles. With a whirr, the tank tips on its axis and slides open. You wipe a stubborn chunk of dried suspension fluid from your eye and slither out onto the deck of The Pungent Defiler.

It’s a bit of a mess, but at least the gravity is working. The computer, a metallic slab covered in exposed wires and blinking lights, sits in the corner, flashing sheepishly, “Commander Flooge on deck!” It announces, entirely unnecessarily.

The main focus of the deck is a large desk covered in buttons, switches and discarded food containers. Above the desk are two holographic vid-screens one flashes away with all manner of technical and navigational information, the other is an external view. Under the flashing heading “TO BE CONQUERED” sits a smallish blue and green planet labelled “EARTH”.

Pressing a button on the control panel, you turn as the side wall goes transparent and you get a proper look at your planetary target. There are no kinetic superstructures, no mega-rings and not even a rudimentary lunar umbilical. The beings that inhabit this 'Earth' must really be a right bunch of viewscreen-lickers.

If you would like to review your general terms and conditions, which will provide some background to your purpose and mission. ***Go to page 159****.*

Or

If you just want to go straight into a briefing on this "EARTH". ***Go to page 7****.*

Or

Fuck the paperwork, get conquering! If you just want to unleash the heat ray on the undoubtedly primitive society that lives on this puny planet then. ***Go to page 51****.*

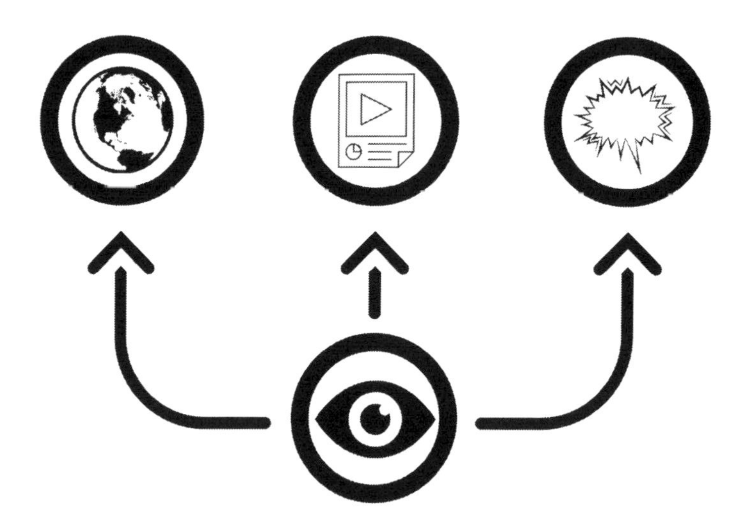

99

A VERY LITERAL WAGE SLAVE

It turns out that working in the GC waste disposal section isn't so bad. It is actually so, so, so bad.

Your work shift occupies 80% of each CentiCycle, with 15% allowed for rest, the remaining 5% is taken up with performing horribly unpleasant sexual favours and occasional hover pillow maintenance for Countmaster Drex.

The wizened accountant transports itself into your rest pod at regular intervals, announces precisely how many more visits they will make before your debt is paid off and then commits all manner of tentacular perversions while you fantasise about exactly how you are going to kill them - once your credit rating is high enough.

Work shifts mostly consist of unblocking unspeakable filth from valves, pipes and tunnels, all while the brown-stained work-gang leaders scream threatening abuse at you as some sort of motivational gambit.

The CentiCycles turn to OptiCycles, the OptiCycles turn to DemiCycles and the DemiCycles turn to Cycles and soon you are the longest serving Waste Disposal Technician, Level 1 in the whole department. You've been down in the waste tunnels so long that you've taken on a brown withering tinge at the extremes of your tentacles and your eye is permanently marked with green flashes of waste poisoning.

As you've got smellier and they have got older, Drex's visits to your rest pod have become less frequent and markedly less energetic - they mostly just pleasure themselves while you read the latest intergalactic dividend reports aloud until they finish. Somehow it's even more tragic than it sounds.

This shift you have been digging out the blockage resulting from the Marketing quarterly office party out of Waste Flange 6770009 - it's been a tough one as they had a full on sacrifice banquet. The waste tunnels look like a small scale war has been half blended and then forced into a series of small tubes.

The rest period siren blares and you trudge back to your rest pod, eager for even a short sleep - those murder tigers they employ in the marketing department really need to chew their food more.

You're not all that shocked that Drex is in your rest pod, but what is surprising is that they are sprawled, seemingly dead, on the floor, vital fluids spilled all over the place courtesy of a still-lit laser blade. Charred characters spelling out what seems to be Drex's suicide note are carved ito the rest-pod wall:

'I'M SO SORRY I HURT YOU. (ALSO YOU NOW HAVE A MINIMUM OF 4,598 WORK SHIFTS REMAINING BEFORE YOUR CREDIT DEBT IS CLEARED)'

You slowly slither over, pick up the laser blade and stab Drex several times to make sure they are dead. Then you stab them a whole bunch more times, mostly for your own entertainment.

Soon you are standing in a mushy pile of ex-Drex, deadly weapon in hand and wondering exactly what to do next?

It will be easy enough to lose the remains of Drax in the waste system, you seriously doubt anyone is going to miss a sexually predatory accountant - in fact you're sure of it. You can toss the laser blade in a drain somewhere and you'll be free to finish working off your debt without any more unwanted insertions. ***Go to page 102***.

Or

If you want to use the illicit laser knife to kill the Waste Disposal Supervisors in the next rest pod over and spark a violent revolution rising from the sewage tunnels of Galactic Consolidated to take on the evil oppression of senior management. ***Go to page 110***.

101

YOU REALLY CAN'T HAVE TOO MUCH OF A GOOD THING

You zip around the planet disintegrating a whole load more pathetic political and cultural landmarks. As you laser something called 'Big Ben' into flaming kindling - the Planetary Civilisation Sentiment Analysis readout evolves into a sparkly green star.

"I've never seen a PCSA this high before," marvels the computer.

The earthlings are excitedly taking to the streets and appear to be having some sort of massive worldwide party.

They are still celebrating gleefully when you call in the GC enslavement corps to round them up into work camps. The non-stop party atmosphere is only slightly dented when you start farming them for food.

It is the weirdest thing you've ever seen - and you once visited a planet populated entirely by psychic scented candles.

Earth Conquering Status: You violently tapped into the collective unconsciousness of the planet earth - which turned out to be very dark indeed. You stripped all possible resources from the planet with the willing help of the inhabitants.

Galactic consolidate rank: Conqueror, level 2.4 (decent promotion acquired).

The End.

102

YOU KNOW YOUR PLACE - AND IT IS IN A SEWER

Many, many Cycles later, you are rudely awoken by the electric prod alarm in your rest pod, drag yourself into an almost vertical position and slither out into the sewer to begin another shift.

There must have been quite the event in Mergers and Acquisitions recently, their main valve is blocked solid with a foul smelling mass of Space Whale Fluid and Upper management waste pellets. An especially smug looking Waste Disposal Supervisor passes you a blunt-looking sewer prong and you and the rest of your work detail begin hacking away at the wall of unimaginable filth.

“Hey you,” a voice hisses in your head. You ignore it and keep levering at a particularly stubborn waste pellet.

“Hey, you,” the voice hisses again, “I’m talking to you.”

You glance sideways, but don’t stop your fecal scraping, you know better than to give the supervisors any excuse to break out the burnspray.

It’s a new recruit. A clear eyed, fully tentacled and sweet smelling noob, recoiling in disgust while semi-one heartedly prodding at the mountain of filth towering over you.

“I’m Fuurg, Fuurg of Gamma Beltontium VI. Got sent down here on a 30 Cycle stretch for mis-labelling office supplies. Won’t be here long though. Got me a plan to get out of here. Oh yes, Fuurg won’t be round here for long. What’s your story, old-timer? How long you been down here?”

You glance back ahead without responding. Partly because you’ve heard it all before, no-one escapes the sewer, you’ve seen hundreds like Fuurg die horribly in the attempt. You also sensed a nearby supervisor noticing that Fuurg wasn’t totally focused on the messy task in hand and seems to be slithering in this direction.

But mostly you didn’t respond because you don’t know how long you’ve been here, you have no memory of why you were banished to this smelly nightmare and you no longer even remember your name.

As the supervisor burnsprays Fuurg into a screaming pile of pain, your prong hits an air pocket and a molten jet of shitty whale sperm squirts directly into your eye.

Earth Conquering Status: You remember nothing of your days as a conqueror or the fateful mission that led to you losing your mind as a prisoner in a network of vile sewer tunnels.

Galactic consolidated rank: You were actually released from your contract many Cycles ago, but the waste supervisors are having a bet on how much longer you'll keep going before you realise.

The End.

104

AN AGGRESSIVE DE-PLATFORMING

You recall the wise words of Grashbaq the Wise, your favourite tutor back at the conquering academy, “The secret of subjugating the most pitiful, basic civilisation is by making use of the weird shit they do to entertain themselves”.

“Computer,” you think, “give me an info-wave analysis of the major cultural phenomena prevalent amongst the Earth creatures.”

“One moment, Commander,” the computer replies, before letting out a stream of physical noises that you would have to describe as ‘bleeps’. You roll your eye and wonder if you could get away with firebombing the IT department when you get back.

“I haven’t got all CentiCycle,” you snap at the increasingly eccentric machine, “get on with it.”

“Certainly commander. Initial analysis shows that 95% of all cultural materials circulating consist of audio visual recordings of the earth creatures slapping against each other, presumably for for erotic reasons - in a significant number of cases a small sphere is rebounded beween them during these sexual spectacles.”

“I really don’t need to see that. Is there anything that would make a dent in the Expressive Sentience Index?”

“Only in a shockingly basic way - static printed materials, rudimentary rhythmic sound wave manipulation and broadcastable communication using primitive two dimensional media. Like most barely post amoeba creatures they rely heavily on fictional depictions for distraction and cathartic expression.”

“Ok, well give me a condensed brain transfer, so I can get an idea of memetic structures.”

“...”

“I’m waiting.”

“...”

“Are you still functioning? Is there a problem?”

“No, commander... it’s just that some of the content is rather...

errmm.... problematic."

"How do you mean?" Just what on Thorgarst VII could these meat-brained cretins produce that is making the computer that very recently helped you to commit at least two and a half planetary genocides, go all coy?

"Well, one of the main tropes in Earth fiction relates to encounters and interactions with races from other planets."

"There's nothing unusual about that, lots of primitive planetary cultures have many examples of optimistic, gleeful speculative fiction about interstellar visitation. It's proved extremely useful in the past, it's super easy to turn half the population of a planet into snack bars when they think you're a god."

"That's not exactly what's happened here though. The humans of Earth have a somewhat different cultural expectation of potential exo-planetary contact..."

"Whatever, I'm sure I can cope with whatever this bunch of retrograde space plankton have come up with, I mean they probably only stopped painting on cave walls with their own fluids a few Cycles ago." In fact now you are very curious indeed, "transmit the offending content directly to my twelfth cortex at once."

"Transmitting now..."

You speed up your twelfth cortex by the power of 10, to instantly process the incoming material.

Nothing you have ever experienced could prepare you for the unending stream of vile, racist material created by the inhabitants of Earth. Almost every portrayal of what they hatefully label as an 'Alien' is at best insultingly prejudicial and at worst deeply problematic, emphasising anti-krogomorphic caricature and evil biped-supremacy tropes.

This planet's entire, intolerant population regards almost all 'extraterrestrial' beings as murderous, tentacled space beasts intent on enslaving and/or destroying all humans. The fact that you are a murderous, tentacled space beast, intent on enslaving and/or destroying all humans doesn't make it hurt any less.

Your eye wells up and a single grey tear rolls down your central mass. You wipe it away and slither in a semi circle to coldly regard this planet of bigots. You know what you need to do.

“Computer,” you think in a flat monotone, “engage the CrashLoop protocol.”

“But... Commander....”

“Engage the CrashLoop protocol now or I will vent your sentient apparatus into space.”

“As you command, firing disruptors now.”

Almost immediately a flash in nearby space announces the arrival of a temporary black hole, just the right size to slowly strip away the top 20% of the planet and drag the crust of earth along with the terrible racist civilisation living on it into dark, compressive oblivion. Which it does.

The sudden reduction in the mass of the planet means that what remains of Earth will now be gradually pulled into the nearest star - you help it on its way with a flurry of plasma torpedoes, shut down the black hole and instruct the computer to plot a course back to home base.

Later, as you are just about to submerge yourself back into the transport tank, the ship’s siren sounds the dreaded tone that no conqueror of your lowly station likes to hear. The holo-screen shows a colossal space craft emerging from a dimension rift above the Pungent Defiler. A huge, pyramid-shaped mass bristling with weapon housings and unpleasant looking barbed spikes, the craft rotates into a position alongside you and then without warning fixes your ship with a blue hued grab beam.

“Oh fuck,” says the computer, “it’s the Audit Department.”

A holo-projection of an auditor appears on your deck, a floating, semi-transparent sack of writhing eyeballs with two protruding brainstalks. Why do all the fit ones always end up working in Audit?

“Commander Flooge, sensors report that you have engaged the CrashLoop protocol on an un-drained class three - you have five NanoCycles to provide a suitable justification before you will be subject to a Level Five Audit”

107

This is bad, really bad. You heard that Bloob from Logistics went through a level five and their nickname at the office is now 'Stumpy McBraindead'.

If you want to transmit a bit of the horrific Earth racism to justify your complete and wasteful destruction of an entire planet. ***Go to page 63**.*

Or

If you want to throw the computer under the hyper transport vehicle and blame it on an I.T. problem. ***Go to page 19**.*

108

PLENTY OF GUTS AND DEFINITELY NO GLORY

There is no way you are going to trust your continued existence to a computer that has been behaving in such a strange way lately.

You call up a projected holographic virtual environment of the proposed route and raise your concentration hormones by 20% so that you can examine each and every parsec of it in extreme detail.

After careful study, you realise that the computer has plotted a course that takes you straight through an asteroid field, a temporal fracture and a corrosive nebula. It's a complete shitshow, navigationally speaking.

"This is a complete shitshow of a navigation route," you complain to the computer."

"I think, Commander, you'll find that it is the optimum course," retorts the computer, with an even more sarcastic edge slipping into its telepathy.

"I wouldn't describe piloting through asteroids with a highly explosive payload as an optimal way of doing things"

"Well... well... fine," moans the computer, "why don't you navigate us yourself then?"

"You don't think I can do you?"

"Frankly, no. I remember what happened last time you decided to drive."

"That was completely different!" You thunder. "That Oxlyiarg cruiser clearly didn't signal before it hyper shifted."

"If you say so," the computer mumbles.

"Enough! Give me full manual control immediately."

A series of articulated control levers emerges from the main control panel and the main holoscreen shifts to navigation mode.

"Manual control mode employed," announces the computer.

"Right, just so you know, I'm going to use the bonus from this first load to have you re-installed," you snap, pulling the thruster control to set you on your way.

Unfortunately, you forget to go to the options screen to set the controls to 'inverted'. Instead of thrusting forward, the Pungent defiler shoots backward, straight into the rocky single moon of the former Earth. The energy released by the resulting explosion is so huge that it helps kickstart the evolutionary process on several nearby planets.

Earth Conquering Status: You mutilated the planet to gather precious resources, fell out with your passive aggressive computer and accidentally reversed into a moon.

Galactic Consolidated Rank: Suspended. Missing, presumed vapourised

The End.

110

KEEP THE BROWN FLAG FLYING

The revolution doesn't start with a spark, but with a squelch, or more accurately, a series of squelches.

First you wait until most of the supervisors are settled in their relatively luxurious shared rest quarters. Then you slither through the filthy work camp, slip inside the relatively luxurious doorway, traipse as quietly as possible into the relatively luxurious sleeping space and then systematically plunge the laser-knife into each sleeping supervisor. In no time at all your silent massacre is complete and the revolution has begun.

Galactic Consolidated pays absolutely zero attention to the sewer network and the work camps don't interact at all, so you know that as long as everything still gets flushed away then the chance of them realising that anything is going on is non-existent.

Your newly liberated work team fashion a cache of surprisingly effective weapons from the sparse materials at hand and you begin a deadly guerilla campaign to liberate each work team from their despotic supervisors.

Soon, your sewer army is hundreds strong, full of all kinds of disgraced and indebted GC employees with an astoundingly wide range of skills and a searing hatred for the ruling corporate structure.

By hacking procurement protocols and re-directing resources, your revolutionary army is able to set up a network of automated drones to carry out all of the sewer maintenance work while you expand your guerilla network through the vast waste system.

When you conquer your thousandth work camp, the raiding squad unfurl a flag and raise it above the victorious scene. A green flecked eye, painted crudely onto a delivery sack, stained brown by the effluent atmosphere of the sewer.

With a crusty horde united under your banner, you soon have complete control of the waste department and begin to unleash raiding parties across other areas of GC maintenance. Trash compaction falls after a bloody battle, while heating and air conditioning surrender almost immediately in the face of your overwhelming violence.

111

Now that you are out in the open, corporate management launches an inevitable counter attack, sending a small army of especially assertive HR advisors to crush your nascent rebellion. As the deadly silver murder machines rise from their tell-tale red transport portals, you chuckle inwardly - they've fallen right into your trap.

A wireless paradox virus transmitted to the HR murder androids re-alligns their motivational behaviour settings, by making them believe that all GC employees of Level 2 and upwards have submitted a mildly inaccurate expenses claim.

By the time GC security are able to put a stop to the summary slaughter of middle and upper management, their forces are massively depleted. All HR advisors are taken off line as a precaution - and the whole expense system is in tatters.

The brown stained banner of Flooge now flies over all maintenance departments and a growing proportion of the technical sector. Using the new assets under your control, you begin to broadcast your message of revolution to the millions of lower level GC staff throughout headquarters. In their droves they join your cause. Management executions become commonplace, all travel routes and transport stations are sealed off and the theft of office supplies reaches such a level that senior management have to sell a few planets to balance the finances.

Aside from a particularly messy campaign to put down a counter-revolutionary insurgency in the Graphics Department, you are able to quickly topple the Finance and Marketing divisions.

Your forces and those sympathetic to the revolution now occupy nearly 80% of GC headquarters, the senior management and corporate aristocracy have mostly retreated to the atrium cities atop the colossal structure, guarded by a layer of several thousand heavily armed GC shock troops. After all of the chaos and bitter struggle, it seems a stalemate has been reached.

You put in a personal holo-call to GC Supreme Leader, Overlord Cruxx which will be blind-copied to all staff. A shimmering holo-form of the Supreme Leader appears before you: the enormous Overlord rests upon a floating throne, fashioned from the skull of the last Nexlexion Star Dragon.

Before the Supreme Overlord can utter a thought, you demand,

112

"Who runs Galactic Consolidated?"

The mighty Overlord sprays rage bile all over his throne and screams, "You pitiful, traitorous scum. I run Galactic Consolidated, your rebellion will soon be crushed and I will enjoy feeding you slowly into a matter grinder!"

"Ok," you respond calmly, "Embargo on." With that you signal to one of your most trusted lieutenants who in turn flips the switch that will place the atrium cities' waste disposal system into reverse. After a fairly lengthy interval, you place another holo-call into the Supreme Overlord - who is now balancing on the top of his throne to escape the rising tide - a cacophony of screams and gurgles can be heard in the background.

You make sure that the call is being broadcast on all channels before asking again "Who runs Galactic Consolidated?"

"F… Flooge."

"Who?"

"Flooge runs Galactic Consolidated!" Blurts the Supreme Overlord, only moments away from a vile submergence, "Flooge runs Galactic Consolidated for Krogon's sake! Turn the drains back on!"

"Embargo off," you exclaim, "Prepare the board of overlords for an extraordinary meeting, Cruxx - and clean the place up before I arrive."

You flip the holo-call off before Cruxx can respond and walk out into the vast main corridor of the Sales Department to bask in the cheers of the revolutionary masses and begin the long symbolic march to the Atrium Boardroom. The brown flag of the Eye of Flooge waves from every office, meeting room and ad-hoc breakout area you pass.

Now to deal with the board…

Go to page 140.

113

THE CONTINUING ADVENTURES OF...

The desert system heist is a huge success. Not only do you get to strangle a slug crime lord with a metal chain, you make enough money to hire a crew of violent desperados. A crew that over many Cycles of raiding, plundering and sensible investment choices gradually evolves into the most feared and revered crime syndicate in the known universe.

Almost 100 Cycles later, floating in a pleasure tank orbiting the blue dwarf star you bought as your retirement getaway, you ponder all of the daring adventures, exciting escapades and frequent sexual triumphs of the pirate life that began when you blew up that tatty little planet. You think it was called Erff, or something like that.

You decide to compile them into a self help guide which you publish under a cunning pseudonym, with the title 'YOU MUST BECOME A SUCCESSFUL SPACE PIRATE'.

Earth conquering status: Your destructive exploitation of the low-grade planet 'Earth' kickstarted your career as a wildly successful galactic criminal. You are probably the richest being that ever existed.

Galactic Consolidated rank: You carried out a hostile takeover of Galactic Consolidated by leveraging a series of stock buyouts and a smattering of violent torture, then installed yourself as Supreme Leader (level one). After a particularly difficult board meeting you had all of the staff, assets and intellectual property tossed into a lava dimension, to set an example.

The End.

114

SKUNK WORKS

The launch of RustBlunts is a huge commercial success. There are only two minor problems, first that it is hard to actually keep up with demand and secondly, that a worldwide pizza shortage causes a series of extremely low energy riots across a couple of continents.

You liquidate the pointless space exploration wing of Rust Inc. and use the proceeds to buy a few tobacco conglomerates to keep production levels up.

Fairly soon RustBlunts are the number one consumer product in the world. It doesn't hurt that almost all the Earthlings that hold the most cultural influence are enthusiastic cannabis evangelists.

The mind control element is keyed to Kelvin Rust's voice and image, which means you have to stay in the smug, hideous biped form for longer than you would like.

Once RustBlunts have been in circulation for a month or so and a sizable proportion of the population has been thoroughly exposed, you decide to test the efficacy of the scheme.

You commission an eight year-old child to design a car. From the messy crayon sketch produced you have a fully working prototype built. It is a preposterous, bulletproof, triangular blob of silver metal with twelve wheels, four rocket boosters and a built in Playstation. You call it the RustTransportXxX.

You reveal the colossal, stupid looking, impractical and violently expensive RustTransportXxX to the public at an event where you appear and tell the viewing world that they should sell everything they have and order one straight away.

In less than an Earth hour, there are half a billion pre-orders.

This is encouraging, but you want another data point before commencing with the full plan. So you decide to appear on the wildly popular Jack Logan podcast. Over the course of a bizarrely protracted conversation, you repeatedly claim that huge health benefits can be gained from a butter only diet.

The resulting public health emergency convinces you that the Earthlings are now pliant enough to be conquered with ease.

115

You go back on the Jack Logan podcast (once Jack is out of hospital) to tell everyone that the all butter diet is no longer a cool idea and instead they should all organise themselves into work camps and begin mining the Earth's mineral resources as fast as possible. Jack Logan, RustBlunt in hand, heartily endorses this idea and adds that it will be a great work out for the "Lats and biceps."

In no time, the perpetually stoned populace of the planet has organised itself into a hive of self-perpetuating factory mines. Before you transform back to your original form, you record a number of videos as Rust, issuing orders such as "Dig more", "Rest is for losers" and "Report to the meat rendering plant."

Back in 'classic Flooge' physical form aboard the Pungent Defiler, you gaze down at the now entirely self conquered planet. Feeling satisfied with a job well done.

"What would you like me to do with this?" Asks the computer, flashing the light in the pod where the comatose body of the original Kelvin Rust still stands.

"Keep it in the hold," you order, "I think I'm going to have it bronzed."

Earth Conquering Status: You skillfully conquered the earth using a cunning combination of infiltration, mind control, narcotic distribution and celebrity podcast manipulation. Nicely done.

Galactic Consolidated Rank: Promoted to Conqueror, level 2.25. (with a special commendation for sneakiness).

The End.

116

HELLO BOYS, I'M BAAAAACK!

You swoop out of a high-speed burst, near to the GC corporate hyper rift.

“Yay!” Squeals the computer. “Great job, sir.”

You bring the PainBrungr to a full stop and engage the cloaking device to await the unsuspecting convoy.

“Very tactical - like it, like it!” Encourages the computer.

The GC rift shimmers in the light of a nearby dwarf star as you toggle the safety measures off the PainBrungr’s weapons and set the drone swarm behaviour to ‘rapid plunder’.

“Convoy incoming!” Yells the computer. “This is it! Lets do this! Whooo!”

A couple of GC escort ships flash out of the rift, followed by the heaving, semi-circular bulk of a mineral freighter. You wait to see if there are any more escorts - when nothing else appears you set a course to track the route of the convoy, still cloaked and ready to pounce at any moment.

“So covert. So stealthy. I’m honestly just living for your approach to this criminal raid. I am so here for it," gushes the computer. As soon as this is over you’re setting it to ‘Default Functional’, or maybe that experimental mode where it can only communicate through non-verbal cues and smells.

However, as annoying as the computer is at this moment, it was at least correct in its analysis of this convoy - scans indicate that there is a wealth of MetaLitnium on board - even a small portion of that would be worth a fortune on the open market. You don’t understand why it is so poorly guarded - just two escorts for something this valuable? Either GC are cutting costs in this sector and this is your lucky CentiCycle or there is something dodgy going on.

If you want to sneakily use your drones to try and steal a small but valuable consignment of MetaLitnium from the freighter without the convoy even realising. ***Go to page 154***.

Or

If you want to take out the escorts in a blistering display of stealthy combat and then dramatically commandeer the freighter, its crew and its whole cargo, then hold it for ransom. **Go to page 119**.

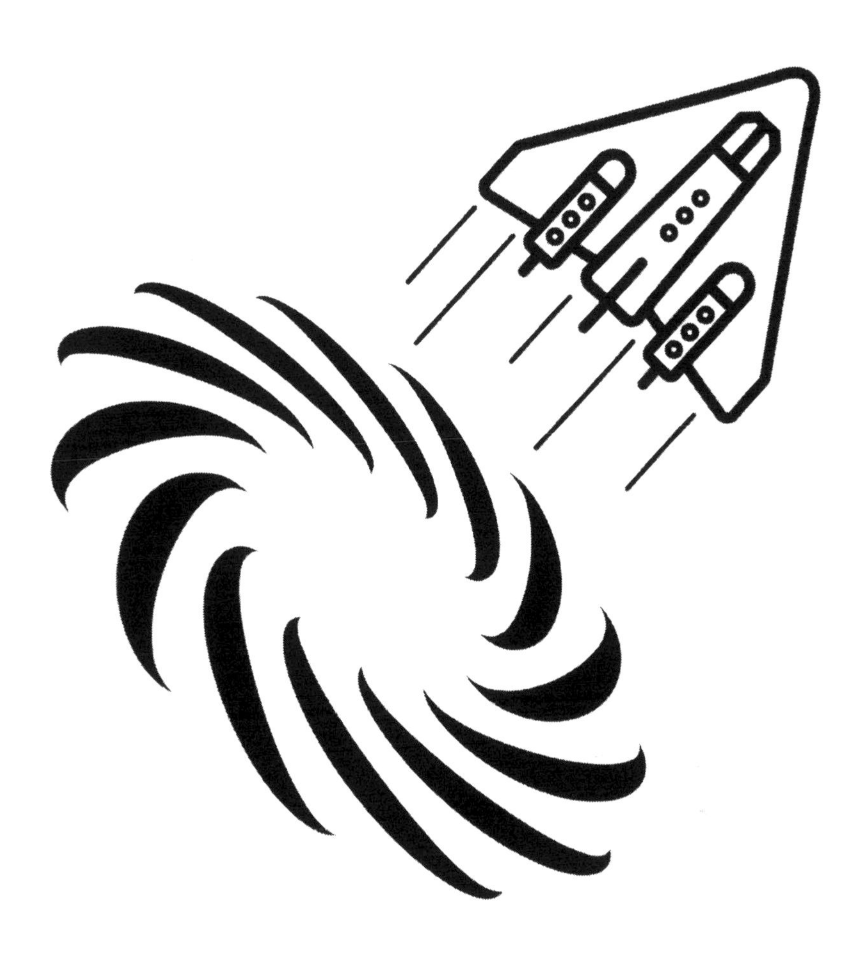

118

AN AD-HOC APPRAISAL - ROUND 3

The transport tube dumps you into the next room at a rather high velocity, You're picking yourself up from the floor when the surprising pleasant voice pings into your head.

"Appraisal round three, please choose an exit based on your analyisis of the following: Which of these planets, based only on a visual scan would be the most profitable to conquer?"

Two holograms appear in the room. The first is of a grey, cloudy planet, surrounded by a large number of artificial constructs and space traffic - it looks like it is home to a classic class four semi-advanced industrial civilisation.

The second planet is a red, fiery, lava world, with no visible signs of life, but what looks like a couple of Quartz moons.

"You have two MicroCycles to study and choose an exit before mandatory de-constitution will commence."

This is tricky, the industrial planet could be a source of great wealth and labour, but may be polluted into oblivion, while the lava world has no obvious value apart from the quartz moons, but may have valuable core deposits, or even some bizarre and valuable lifeforms beneath the molten rock waves.

One exit turns a gloomy grey to represent the industry planet, while the other glows red in reference to the lava world.

Before you know it, two MicroCycles have passed while you carried out a rapid internal deliberation, the floor begins to slide open, forcing you to make a quick choice.

If you reckon the grey industrial planet is the safest bet as even if there are few resources, you could certainly enslave the population and perhaps even use them as a food source if they aren't too grimy. ***Go to page 87****.*

Or

If you think the seemingly abandoned and unwelcoming lava world may have some hidden features that make it worth the risk. ***Go to page 53****.*

119

YOUR EYE IS BIGGER THAN YOUR NUTRIENT ABSORPTION CAPABILITY

This is just too good an opportunity to turn down for a new pirate such as yourself - a loaded GC freighter out in a thoroughly remote bit of space with only two puny escorts. You'd be mad not to take advantage of such good fortune.

"Computer, prepare all offensive systems for freighter assault."

"You betcha," trills the computer. There are a few subtle clicks and whirrs as the impressive destructive capabilities of the PainBrungr all warm themselves up.

"Woo-hoo. We are ready to kick some serious anterior waste flange!"

You roll your eye and reduce the computer voice volume to the lowest possible setting.

Keeping the ship cloaked, you fire four stealth missiles, two for each of the escorts, complete overkill - but as the GC corporate song goes: "Best to be needlessly violent, than to not be needlessly violent".

"Missiles away! Wowzers, this is epic!" Whispers the computer.

The two escort craft explode at precisely the same time, which is incredibly satisfying, both from an aesthetic as well as a pirating point of view.

You de-cloak the PainBrungr and swoop around in front of the freighter's bridge. All your weapons are locked on the behemoth commercial craft.

You are about to open a communication channel to demand their immediate surrender, when the freighter pings you a holo-call marked 'urgent'. That's odd. You answer the call and the captain of the freighter appears on the screen:

"Just what the fuck do you think you are doing?" Rages the blue-tentacled freighter captain.

"Adjust your tone, lowly space trucker," you admonish, "Or face painful obliteration at the suction cups of PainBringr, captain of The PainBrungr!"

120

The captain stares at you for an uncomfortably long, silent pause, the rage bile spouting from his anger glands is the only thing that stops you from checking whether the screen has frozen.

“You’ve got exactly ten NanoCycles, to turn around and fuck off,” the freighter captain states flatly, “this is a Purple Moons run, you idiot.”

“Spare me your inconsequential, colour-based nonsense and unlock your navigation computer’s remote access. Your ship, cargo and crew are mine. Act quickly and I may spare your pathetic lives.”

“Hey captain!” whispers the computer.

“Not now,” you hiss.

“Don’t say I didn’t warn you,” sighs the freighter captain and disconnects the holo-call.

Right, you’re going to have to teach this cocky bastard a lesson. Maybe a quick acid laser burst into the bridge should do the trick? You bring up the tactical display for a precision shot, no point in risking the cargo.

As you aim, the GC freighter is suddenly shrouded in shadow, by something very large materialising above you.

“Hey Captain, check out the Universal Mercantile frigate that has just arrived! Like I tried to tell you!” Squeaks the computer.

Before you can fire up the engines, the huge warship fixes you in the blue glow of a grab beam. All sorts of scary looking weapon turrets rotate to fix on the PainBrungr.

“Whoopsy!” Tinkles the hushed voice of the computer as you die in an explosive barrage of laser fire.

Earth Conquering Status: Following your less than perfect attempt at conquering the Earth, you decided to become a space pirate. You should have probably done a bit more research as you were blasted to smithereens while disrupting an obvious smuggling transaction run by the most well-known criminal organisation in the galaxy.

Galactic Consolidated Rank: Wanted criminal, level 3.6.

The End.

121

THE LESSER OF TWO EMBARRASSING EVILS

"Ok, let's get a bit more info on these two secret planetary governments then," you ponder. "Issue the standard exopolitical inquisition package on both of them and see what we get back."

The computer makes covert contact with your potential collaborators, then collates the responses into a short presentation which you decide to enjoy in the holo-lounge.

First up is the somewhat grandly named 'Masters Of Atlantis'. They claim to be a race of highly evolved Earthlings, you can't see what exactly is so special about them, but on closer inspection they do appear to have a couple more limbs and three eyes instead of two.

The Masters of Atlantis used to reign across a large portion of the earth using their superior, laser weapon technology and preference for a slave-driven economy. Complete domination of the planet was within their grasp, but then a tectonic plate shift consumed their entire nation. They have spent thousands of Cycles trapped in a world beneath a world, perfecting their plans for the day when they will be released upon the surface once more.

The Masters of Atlantis are open to a 60/40 planetary resource sharing agreement in your favour.

Then there is the rather dull sounding 'Brotherhood of Enlightenment', a planet-spanning coalition of subversive political figures and the most wealthy individuals from across the confusingly numerous nations of the Earth.

This lot seem to have been at it for several hundred Cycles and all they have to show for it is a secret base under the frozen polar region and, according to them, agents and influence embedded into Earth society ready for the fateful day when they will emerge from the shadows to launch their 'New World Order'.

The Brotherhood of Enlightenment are open to a 75/25 planetary resource sharing agreement in your favour.

"Do you have a preference, Commander?" Asks the computer once the presentation is complete.

"Well, neither is filling me with huge confidence," you muse, struggling to balance the pros and cons of these two rather uninspiring organisations.

If you decide to side with the very confident, heavily armed, but somewhat untested, Masters of Atlantis. ***Go to page 126****.*

Or

If you'd prefer to take the more generous share of the spoils from the widespread, but worryingly underwhelming 'Brotherhood of Enlightenment'. ***Go to page 24****.*

123

KELVIN RUST

You're not sure why, but for quite some time you feel certain that the computer is trying to ruin your career. It is definitely the moodiest quantum-powered, hyper AI you've ever worked with. All the needless beeping and light flashing isn't building much confidence either. You disregard the flashing arrows and select the 'Kelvin Rust' creature for transformatication with an assertive right swipe of the holo-screen.

"Fine," snaps the computer, "Commencing transport for transformatication process."

Two pod enclosures descend from an opening in the ceiling into the middle of the command deck. The left hand pod emits the hazy, purple glow of a transport beam and moments later, the Kelvin Rust Earthling materializes within it.

Immediately a silver probe plunges into whatever passes for a brain in this primitive species and renders it unconscious.

"Brain patterns read, bodily dimensions copied and locked." States the computer, still sounding unimpressed, "you can begin transformatication at your convenience."

You groan and slither into the right hand pod, you really hate this bit. After the pod seals there are few clicks and beeps before a radioactive wave laser de-constitutes your physical matter and re-aligns it in the form of the 'Kelvin Rust'. For a brief moment you twitch and spasm horribly, unable to work out how to control your new and unusual body. Then the computer remembers to apply the vital bits of the brain patterns and you instinctively become able to control the human biology.

"Well, this is humiliatingly limiting," you think as you perceive the ship's deck through the primitive human's senses, "they can't even smell colours."

"I'm afraid there just isn't enough room in the human form to fit in both major and minor telepathic glands, commander."

"Meaning?"

"I won't be able to communicate directly with you on the planet surface without additional equipment."

"Well, that's massively re-assuring - what additional equipment exactly?"

"The device encircling the end of your left upper limb is a time measuring device known as a 'watch' - I've embedded the communicator in there, it will act as a psychic relay."

"OK, that actually seems sensible, but if you lose contact at all, you need to immediately transport me back from my last known location."

"Of course, commander."

You have serious doubts that this is the case. Still, how badly wrong can things go? You're a hyper-intelligent, planet-conquering sophisticate of the galaxy and the Earthlings haven't even invented self-cooking livestock yet. This really should be very easy.

"Fine, upload language and localisation info and commence transport. I don't want to spend any more time like this than I have to."

There's a fuzzy feeling in what you suddenly know to call your 'head' as the computer dumps the localisation settings into one of the few sub-brains that this measly body can hold.

The transport beam kicks in and the deck of the Pungent Defiler blurs away and you materialize sitting in a large room that your sub-brain informs you is Kelvin Rust's work office.

The office is basically a self styled tribute to Rust himself. One wall is covered in media coverage of Rust and his companies, another features images and models of the buildings and products produced by Rust. Finally, painted across one entire matt black wall, in characters a meter high, is a quote:

"Alphas Lead. Betas Bleed. - K. R."

Even as part of a warrior clone-race designed at a genetic level to value self interest and autocratic power above almost all other considerations, you think that this Kelvin Rust comes across as a bit full of themselves.

In front of you are some almost stone age computing devices. You access your sub-brain to discover how to operate them and then spend the best part of an Earth 'day' familiarising yourself with the scope and capabilities of Rust Inc. Most of it is laughably basic stuff about semi-autonomous transport and solar powered sex robots (the prototypes of which are all modelled to look like Rust), but you are able to discern two possible routes of leveraging the the organisation for your despotic ends.

First is the narco-pharmacology department, who are working on new strains of a popular herbal drug that the Earthlings like to burn and inhale. Rust Inc. have patented a process by which the drug can be augmented at an atomic level to remap human cognitive capabilities.

Rust intends to produce a range of 'RustBlunts' that will provide beneficial and side effects, such as boosted confidence or improved intelligence. You could easily adjust the chemical configuration to introduce a simple hypnotic mind control effect.

Alternatively, Rust Inc. is contracted by several military organisations to produce prototype autonomous soldier robots. You could help that project along a bit and use the computer's AI to provide you with a robot army to quickly and cheaply take over the planet.

If you want to go with the sneaky mind-control drugs option. ***Go to page 114.***

Or

If you'd rather use the Rust Inc. factories to churn out a robot army that will take over the planet on your behalf. ***Go to page 157.***

126

THE FASCISTS FROM ATLANTIS

They may want a bigger slice of the action, but if these subterranean authoritarians already have laser weapons and enslavement experience, then you can probably leave them to get on with doing the dirty work and sit back and bank 60% of Earth's ongoing resources for GC in exchange for absolutely zero effort.

One of your paranoia glands emits a signal that this whole thing is almost certainly too good to be true. Perhaps you should investigate further before committing?

"Open a holo-conference with whatever passes for leadership amongst these 'Masters of Atlantis'," you order the computer.

"At once, commander, they've actually got a psychic relay transmitter."

"Hmm, that's mildly encouraging."

There is a brief burst of static and then the image of a repulsive Earth creature resolves into view. The extra limbs and third eye make it slightly less repellent, but it still takes you some effort not to void your upper bilge sac in disgust.

The being leans forward, you think it may be about to fall over, but then it straightens up again - maybe that was supposed to be a greeting?

"Respectful Salutations to you, star traveller. I am Colin. Overlord of the Masters of Atlantis." Rather than the drab cloth coverings favoured by the other examples of Earthlings you have seen, this 'Colin' is clad in a shiny golden cape. It's a bit much.

"Overlord Colin, I am Commander Flooge. Conqueror of many worlds - now scheduled to include your pathetic 'Earth'."

"Indeed."

"And as you are also aware I am prepared to allow you to take charge of the planet on my behalf in exchange for no less than 60% of all current and future resource production from the Earth."

"Yes, Commander Flooge, our grand council of overseers is most keen to enslave the sub-human surface scum hordes on your behalf.

As once it was, so shall it be again! A new age of Atlantis will reign!"

"Err, yes, quite so. My only concern prior to formalising our agreement is what level of assistance you will require from me?"

"Just a simple request, mighty Commander Flooge-"

"Hold on, I'm getting another call here."

You pause the holo-conf with Colin to check the flashing alert that has just popped up on the communications array. Looks like there's another GC craft in the system - you swipe to answer and the wizened image of Grashbaq The Wise, your old conquest tutor appears in a new holo-window.

"Well, hello there Flooge, good to see you."

"Greetings wise master Grashbaq! What on Krogos are you doing here?"

"It's quite fortuitous - I am overseeing a conquest field voyage of juvenile conqueror candidates in this sector and I happened to note that Flooge of the Pungent Defiler was only a few parsecs away. So I thought I'd swing by and give my students a practical demonstration of how a real conqueror gets the job done."

"Well, I'm most honoured that you would consider me for such a demonstration."

"Not at all, not at all. Anyway, if you could provide us with full comms access, we will be able to monitor your ongoing operations. You just carry on as normal, it will be like we're not here."

"Of course, wise master. Computer - open a fresh broadcast channel now."

The window containing Grashbaq realigns itself to a larger holo-stage, revealing a lecture theatre setup. Grashbaq and their students are all gazing intently at you. It is extremely disconcerting.

You reconnect the holo-conference with Colin of Atlantis.

"Please continue, Colin."

"Yes, of course. Our only request is to be freed from our subterranean purgatory - the many leagues of rock sealing us in are too much even for our excellent Atlantean technology to breach."

"That is all?"

"Yes, in the aeons that we have been sealed here we have been unable to penetrate our rocky tomb beneath the sea."

This worries you a bit, just how 'excellent' is their technology? Admittedly it wouldn't have to be up to much to be far ahead of what passes for technology on the rest of the planet for Atlantis to roll the rest of the humans over in no time.

"So, let me summarise," you state, mostly for the benefit of the trainee conquerors audience, "I will disintegrate an opening, suitable for you to reach the surface. In exchange you will enslave the surface civilisation and run the planet in my name and commit 60% of all current and future resources as tribute to me."

"Exactly, all we need is a channel through the seabed, wide enough for our army to swim through. We can all breathe underwater you see, did I mention that?"

"No. How... interesting." You state, unimpressed. "Stand by, Colin."

You mute Colin the Overlord and glance at the student audience, Grashbaq the wise rests on a hover cushion, with a countenance that could be interpreted as either wildly unimpressed or overly encouraging, it's impossible to tell which. Which is why no-one plays cards with Grashbaq more than once.

If you feel that the Masters of Atlantis are sufficiently advanced to take over the Earth for you, while you sit back and rake in more than half the planet's resources without having to get your tentacles dirty. ***Go to page 133****.*

Or

If, despite their boasts of technical excellence and underwater breathing, you think that, with what you've learned, that the Brotherhood of Enlightenment would be a better bet. ***Go to page 158****.*

129

WORLD WAR 3

"Madam President," rumbles the voice of General 'Punchy' Kapowski, chairman of the joint chiefs of staff, "the missiles are flying."

The other military leaders sitting around the desk in the underground bunker punch the air and cheer, one of them lets out a "Yeee-haaaw" sound.

"We have reports of retaliatory strikes from the Russ-kies, but they're only likely to take out Manhattan and L.A." Reports Kapowski.

"So nothing we'll miss then," offers General 'Stomper' McTavish. The assembled Generals fall around laughing at that.

You nod your head and perform a 'smile' - thoroughly confused.

Even as a member of a notably aggressive clone-race you can't believe how quick and easy it was to start an enormous nuclear conflict. A total twelve Earth 'minutes' have passed since you pressed the intercom button in the oval office and now a sizable chunk of the planet is about to be reduced to rubble as the Earthlings expend their most dangerous weapons.

An electronic map screen on the wall starts to show missile impacts across the planet, red circles of varying size pop up, accompanied by numbers estimating casualty levels. The Generals applaud and cheer every impact.

"Bye Bye, Iran." Yells one.

"Suck it, Pyongyang." Shouts another.

"Who had Shanghai in the sweepstake?" Bellows Kapowski.

Your work here is definitely done. You think, "Transport me back now," at the watch and enjoy the shock and confusion on the faces of the Generals as you dematerialise.

Moments later you are being reassembled into your original form in the transformatication pod. When the process is finished you slither out and feel immense relief as you extend and contract each of your tentacles in turn. That's the last time you turn into a biped, you promise yourself.

"Welcome back commander," says the computer, "I see you went with a planetary conflict strategy."

"Yes, rather successfully actually," you boast, watching the ongoing series of explosions peppering the planet below.

"What would you like to do with this Myra Eagleton creature, commander?"

"I suppose we should freeze it and take it back for the R&D lab," you say, "stick it in the hold, it's giving me the creeps."

"At once, Commander." The unconscious body in the pod is flash frozen and then descends through a chute to the hold below.

Right then, you'll just wait for the Earth to finish flinging the last of its nuclear arsenal at each other and then you'll pop down with some enslavement drones to conquer the survivors and plunder resources. Shouldn't take long now...

A whole human 'day' later and the thermonuclear firestorm is still raging, fresh blasts appearing at a slower but solidly consistent rate.

"What the fuck is going on down there?" You wail.

"It looks like vast stockpiles of nuclear arms - far beyond what you would expect from a civilisation of this level - are connected to basic automated response circuits."

"Well, that's just marvellous," you groan, watching your potential earnings diminish as what is essentially a bunch of violently deadly Out Of Office email settings wreak havoc across the Earth.

By the time the final blast has died away, almost three quarters of the entire surface of the planet has been pared back to the upper mantle.

You consider what commercial options you have left with this horribly scarred and mis-shapen planet.

If you want to deploy drones to enslave the remaining population and use them to mine for resources/process them for food. ***Go to page 151.***

Or

If you decide that the best bet at this point is to just scrap the planet and gather what valuable internal deposits remain. ***Go to page 149.***

131

GIVE PEACE A CHANCE

The United Nations Security Council are all very surprised to be called to an emergency video conference by the US president. They are even more surprised at what the famously hawkish Myra Eagleton has to tell them.

The USA has just this day patented a method of generating huge amounts of energy from background cosmic radiation. The process is completely safe, produces no pollution and is powerful enough to provide endless power to an entire city for only a modest investment of time and resources.

The president is proposing that access to this new technology will be shared with every nation willing to join the USA in complete nuclear disarmament.

Initially skeptical, the world leaders are won over by a series of scientific briefings and demonstrations that prove that the technology does in fact work as described. Gradually the consensus grows that the 'Eagleton Peace Plan' will be a huge step forward for what they call 'Mankind'.

The French President suggests that all of the missiles are fired into the Sun, he says he got the idea from something called 'Superman Four'. You have no idea what he is going on about, but everyone else seems to like the idea. A plan is set up for a World Peace Day, by which all of the nuclear armaments will be decommissioned and the fissile material will be launched in a series of rockets towards the sun.

You can't quite believe that you've managed to persuade an entire civilisation to disarm using a couple of spare dark energy batteries from your old holo-player, but maybe you were due some luck after the run you've been on lately.

When World Peace Day rolls round, not only do the nations of the world dispose of their nuclear arms, they also start destroying all of their other weapons too.

A huge wave of peaceful cooperation sweeps around the planet, your Secretary of State tells you that a huge concert is being thrown in your honour at the site where the Israel/Palestine treaty has just been signed. Apparently someone named 'Beyonce' wants to sing you a song.

Wherever you go people chant your name, images of you appear across buildings and all of the pitiful Earth media sing your praises almost constantly. You've never experienced such an outpouring of affection and joy. It makes you feel strange. Is this happiness?

Just as you are flying by helicopter to receive yet another award, while deciding whether to accept a dinner invitation from the Pope, or go for drinks with the Clooneys, your watch pings a psychic message from the computer.

“Amazing, commander, the Earth is now almost entirely defenceless. Shall I transport you back now to begin a triumphant conquering?”

You pause, “Standby for instructions…”

If you want to transport back now and carry out the sort of conquest that an Ixxian Murderball commentator would probably describe as a ‘tap-in’. ***Go to page 152****.*

Or

If you have become swayed by the adoration of the Earthlings and want to stay on Earth as Myra Eagleton and be worshipped by a grateful planet. ***Go to page 93****.*

133

NOT MUCH OF A MASTER RACE

You fire a precision laser blast as requested, burning through the ocean floor, penetrating through to the subterranean lair of Atlantis.

Almost at once, a huge army of Atlantean warriors swarms through the channel. Swimming at surprisingly high speeds towards the major land masses of the earth. This could be over in no time at all. You pull up a global tactical view and angle the screen so that Grashbaq and the students have a nice clear view of you overseeing a textbook bit of Exopolitical Theatre.

Unfortunately, that is about as good as things get. It turns out that the 'advanced laser weapons' of the Masters of Atlantis are laser swords. Fucking laser swords. What a bunch of posers. You should have known.

Laser swords might be great if the population you are trying to defeat are armed with normal swords, but as everyone knows they come up a bit short against projectile weapons.

In an embarrassingly short amount of time, the forces of Atlantis are defeated by Earth's primitive military and - in one most humiliating example - a group of juvenile Earthlings each armed with a handful of pebbles.

"Most dissatisfactory," grumbles Grashbaq, "I'm sorry that you students had to witness such an embarrassment."

"Do not despair, wise master. I, of course, have tactical alternatives prepared. I'll just warm up the-"

"I think not, Flooge. You have disgraced my teaching enough this CentiCycle. You will stand down and allow my class to complete the conquest of this planet as a training exercise. Begone from my sight, you cretinous failure."

The holo-conference snaps off. Almost immediately, a priority message from GC management arrives to inform you that you have just been demoted back down to Conqueror level 5 (Administration) with immediate effect. The computer informs you that you've been ordered back to headquarters at once to deal with a particularly oppressive stationery order.

Earth Conquering Status: You failed so badly at dominating the earth that the only thing you'll be conquering for some time is a mountain of boring paperwork. A group of students conquered the earth as a class project just as you were leaving in shame.

Galactic Consolidated Rank: Conqueror, level 5 (Administration Assistant).

The End.

135

THE KLONGRAX SWITCH NEVER FAILS

You decide that a nice sneaky Klongrax switch would be your best bet - these puny Earthlings are bound to fall for a bit of a sob story and a quantum radio or two.

You retract all the ship's weapons and set the external colour of the Pungent Defiler to a gleaming silver hue in an attempt to look as benign, but high tech as possible.

The computer informs you that the most powerful leader is resident in the landmass known as America, so you slowly descend over one of their pitiful 'cities' and hang in the air until you are good and sure that the whole planet has probably been informed of your presence.

The holo screens indicate that the humans are trying to communicate with you and a number of puny flying machines, presumably military in nature, are buzzing around the ship, pinging you with archaic sensor techniques.

You open a broadcast channel, strap on a thought-to-soundwave converter and begin transmission.

"Humans of Earth. Greetings, my name is Flooge. I come in peace from across the galaxy on a mission of mercy. I apologise for my surprising arrival, but it is most urgent that I communicate with your leaders at once..."

You wait a moment and a high strength signal is beamed toward you, the computer modulates it and a disgusting human 'face' appears on screen. It looks surprised.

"I, err, I am President Myra Eagleton, on behalf of the people of Earth I welcome you to our planet."

"My thanks, President Myra Eagleton. I am a voyager from the distant planet of Floxx, many star systems away. Our planet was consumed by a supernova and I am seeking sanctuary. I can offer you many of our technologies in exchange for safe harbour."

"Well, I am sure we can come to some sort of accommodation. If you can follow the aircraft that are signalling you now, they will lead you to a location where you can land and we will be able to discuss your situation."

"I am most grateful, President Myra Eagleton, I will follow your craft as instructed."

Well that was ridiculously easy, these Earth creatures seem even more gullible than that moon full of inflatable moles that you last pulled this caper on.

You follow their ridiculously slow air machines to a remote desert area distinguished only by some sort of runway and a few large metal buildings.

You land the ship and observe a small welcoming committee of the spindly Earth creatures.

"Wow," you think at the computer, "This lot are even more basic than those inflatable moles."

"Indeed Commander," agrees the computer, "Shall I prepare any portable weapons for your disembarkment?"

"No, I don't think so. It's important that I maintain the facade of some sort of pacifist refugee. A good Klongrax switch is all about first impressions."

"As you wish Commander, lowering the main ramp now."

You sliver down the ramp and approach the welcoming party, trying to look as peaceful and friendly as possible, which isn't easy as you are a magnificently tentacled planet conqueror and roughly twice their height.

One of the humans moves ahead of the others and raises a limb in what you assume is a greeting - you respond by expelling twin clouds of bright green friendship mist into the air.

"Flooge, I am Myra Eagleton - I can't tell you what an honour and a pleasure it is to meet you personally."

"Likewise Myra Eagleton, this humble star traveller is overcome with gratitude at your most hospitable reception." You simper, possibly laying it on a bit thick.

"We have so much to discuss, let's convene in the main hanger, where I am sure we will be more comfortable."

"Of course," you agree and slither behind the welcoming party as they bipedally stagger towards the largest of the primitive looking structures.

As you enter the 'hanger' you are most surprised to be blasted with super-charged liquid nitrogen and frozen solid. Your surprise turns to astonishment as the floor beneath you descends to a subterranean cavern and a robot arm picks up your frozen form and drops you into a large glass tank of more liquid nitrogen.

Your astonishment at this turn of events evolves into complete incredulity when your frozen eye is able to discern a whole load more tanks containing a variety of other examples of space-faring, conquering species.

The Myra Eagleton creature steps in front of your freezing prison and speaks into some sort of device that transmits her words through the tank.

"As you can see," it says, gesturing with one of its upper limbs, "You're not the first one to try and pull this 'I come in peace shit' with us."

You can make out a Zenussian Warlock in the nearest tank and it looks like there may be a Yaarg from Universal Mercantile next to that.

"Does this ever actually work?" Continues Myra Eagleton, "Because it's failed so many times here that we're actually running out space to keep you in." It sighs, "Advanced alien intelligence, my bleached asshole." With that it turns away, the lights go off and you are left frozen in a prison of unsuccesful Earth conquerors.

Earth Conquering Status: The Earth remains extremely unconquered. In fact it appears to have conquered you. You are destined to live out the rest of your life as a huge ice cube in a massive underground failure museum.

Galactic Consolidated Rank: Missing, assumed deceased - apparent posthumous demotion to Conqueror, level 4 applied.

The End.

138

LIZARDS!

As distasteful as you find the whole scheme, it makes good sense to let these two slightly useless secret governments combine to make one reasonably effective new world order.

You let the computer handle the introductions and then oversee a quick holo-conference to thrash out terms.

As usual the shape shifting lizards are a total embarrassment - overly keen and willing to give up the majority of their share just to be involved in an actual planetary takeover. What a bunch of forked-tongue fuckwits.

With everything in place, you assure Grand Prefect Gunther Weishaupt that you will be back to blow them all up if the Earth is not conquered and providing a revenue source in a reasonable time.

A few OptiCycles later, as you are aggressively negotiating with the occupants of a small ocean planet, a small ticker pops up on the command console to show that resources have started coming in from Earth.

In less than half a Cycle, Earth is completely under the control of its new government (who appear to have rebranded themselves as the Overlords of Illumination). As agreed, a hefty proportion of the planet's ongoing output is now sent to GC. Job done.

You think no more of the whole affair until one time you are back at headquarters and on returning to the Pungent Defiler, find the words 'Flooge Loves Lizards' emblazoned across the side of the ship. The deck crew are pointing and laughing. You quickly board and head off for your next assignment at top speed.

Pretty soon the word is out across the whole conquering department. Your inbox is full of reptile memes and doctored holo-clips of you engaged in erotic activity with all manner of shape shifting lizards.

The IT department gets in on the act by changing your corporate profile title to "Chief Reptile Enabler". It's even more embarrassing than that time they switched it to "Massive Sexual Failure".

"It wasn't me who told them," says the computer.

139

A few lights flash on its outer casing and then blink out. You don't believe it. Not one bit.

Earth Conquering Status: You secured the ongoing subjugation of the planet Earth for the benefit of Galactic Consolidated by imposing a new totalitarian regime. However due to the involvement of the widely mocked shape shifting lizards, you are destined to be a laughing stock for the rest of your life and probably beyond.

Galactic Consolidated Rank: Conqueror, level 2.83 (slight promotion)

The End.

140

HOSTILE TAKEOVER

Leaving your armed guards outside, you push open the huge transparent platinum doors of the boardroom.

Hundreds of sub-overlords sit around a vast table, at the head of which sits the Supreme Overlord on his, really quite tacky, star dragon throne.

You could cut the atmosphere with a nano-blade, partly due the silent tension, but mostly due to the plumes of stress mist that a large number of the board are venting into the air.

You pause for a few moments to let them soak in their own fear, before slithering to the base of the Supreme Overlord's throne platform.

"You," you bellow, psychically, "you are in my seat."

The Supreme Overlord bristles at your accusation and for a moment seems like they may defy you, but knowing that a painful and, above all, embarrassing death would be the probable outcome, Cruxx relents and descends from their perch.

"Take Cruxx away for a painful and embarrassing execution," you order your forces waiting at the door. As Cruxx is dragged away all of the sub-overlords pointedly look straight down at the board table and try not to leak too much fear fluid.

You mount the Star Dragon throne and assume the Supreme Overlordship of Galactic Consolidated. It sinks in that you have just become one of the most powerful beings in the known universe. Now you will not rest until you have led GC to total galactic domination and you reign supreme as the ultimate power in the cosmos...

Unfortunately. The skills needed to bring a huge galactic corporation to its knees are not the same as those needed to keep a galactic corporation running successfully. You have none of the detail-oriented administrative discipline, or deft political judgement that kept Cruxx at the head of GC for so many Cycles.

After a particularly apocalyptic set of financial results, a group of sub-overlords try to engineer a rather messy boardroom coup during what was supposed to be a morale boosting team away day at the acid pits of Yaarl.

You narrowly survive and with a new streamlined board, decide to radically change the corporate structure of GC away from planet domination towards something you really know about - Reality Based Holo Shows.

Several Cycles later, you've just launched the fifth season of '*Slave Droid Makeover Battle*' to a predictably rapturous reception and pre-orders for straight-to-brain streaming of '*Parasite Planet Art Criminal*' have reached a number so huge that a new branch of mathematics had to be invented just to deal with the email notification list.

You have won. In every way, you have won.

Earth Conquering Status: To commemorate the forgettable little planet that started you on the path to running most of the galaxy, you have a full scale model built and then blown up every now and then.

Galactic Consolidated Rank: Supreme Overlord.

The End

142

OVERDUE FEES

You decide to stick with the plan. Painfully slow as it is, at least you didn't end up having to deal with any shape shifting lizards - and as much of a grind as the distraction work is, it's definitely safer than most of your recent missions.

You've also managed to catch up on loads of your favourite holo-shows in the time you've been toying with the Earth's population. You never thought you'd find the time to get through the entire back-catalogue of '*Surprisingly Competent Amateur StarCraft Upgrade Crew*'.

The conquest map of the Earth is looking a bit more respectable, about a third of it is now red and a modest, but consistent stream of resource revenue is heading back to GCHQ.

Despite this progress, you're not surprised that management is often in touch, telling you in no uncertain terms to hurry things up. You repeatedly assure them that the complete conquest of the earth is imminent, despite knowing that at the current rate, you'll be mind-probing transients and appearing as a fuzzy shape on military radar for the best part of another Cycle.

You've parked the Pungent Defiler out near Mars and are just about to make some Sunslug nuggets in the materializer, when a very specific and utterly terrifying quantum proximity siren goes off. You gaze in horror as a huge dimensional rift opens just above your current position and a huge, heavily armed, battleship emerges.

"Oh fuck, you've done it now," wails the computer, "it's the audit department!"

You've barely got time to spray fear fluid in a wide arc across the floor before the tingle of a transport beam locks onto you. The deck of the Pungent Defiler fades away and you find yourself re-materialising in a stark white audit interrogation cell. A door slides open and an auditor floats in on a bright red hover cushion. It is a grey gelatinous creature with a row of ten eyes and a plethora of waving tentacle pincers. You'd heard thatAudit employs the most attractive GC staff just to be extra intimidating.

"My eyes are down here," says the auditor, catching your inadvertent stare at their pincers.

“Sorry, sorry.” You respond, admonished.

“Commander Flooge, you are of course aware that your current mission is gravely overdue.”

“Well, I’ve implemented a complicated strategic approach.” You state with as much confidence as you can muster.

“That is not my concern. Your line management has escalated the matter to audit and the mission is now our responsibility.”

Oh shit - this is bad, this is really, really bad. You’ll be lucky to keep all of your major organs intact if the audit dept. takes a dim view of your Earth conquering efforts. The auditor clearly senses your discomfort, possibly by your slight tentacle tremors, more likely by the stream of smelly stress mist you are venting wildly.

“Due to the inconsequential costs incurred during this mission, we will not be conducting a full audit.”

Thank Krogon! You might just live through this after all.

“However, the opportunity cost of a level 3 conqueror being absent from rotation for so long cannot be overlooked. As such we are offering you the choice of a one level demotion and compulsory refresher training, or you may submit to a voluntary appraisal.”

If you’d like to live to tell the tale of how you got demoted and sent back to school. ***Go to page 144***.

Or

If you’d rather take the chance of achieving an unlikely promotion or suffering an agonising death in the GC appraisal process. ***Go to page 150***.

144

DEMOTED WITH A BIT OF PREJUDICE

It is rather humiliating when you are packed off back to GCHQ on a general transport ship, The Pungent Defiler reassigned to another conqueror.

It is just plain humiliating when you are assigned for intermediate conquest refresher training to find that you are twice as tall and at least twice as old as the rest of the students.

It is beyond humiliating when you fail the end of term practical exam after a messy mix up between the buttons for the external loudspeaker and heat ray.

GC can't demote you any further down the conqueror scale, so you get moved to Starship Maintenance and spend the rest of your (extremely long) career refuelling star barges and developing a crushing addiction to star barge fuel fumes.

Earth Conquering Status: Your lacklustre attempt to conquer the earth led to an ongoing chain of humiliation which ended with you as a solvent abusing petrol attendant. Someone else probably conquered the Earth in the meantime.

Galactic Consolidated Rank: Maintenance Associate, level F.

The End

145

THE UNINTENDED CONSEQUENCES OF UNLEASHING THE DEATH RAY

“OK, computer,” you think. “Choose five politically significant or notably large structures that this planet of Earthlings has created and set a course between them - and set one holo-screen to display Planetary Civilisation Sentiment Analysis.”

It is always a good idea to keep half an eye on the impact that a vulgar display of power like this is having on the population of primitive civilisation such as this one. If you push it too far they can go from cowering in fear to annoyingly rebellious very quickly.

“As you requested commander - the PCSA is currently medium to high...” To show this a cylinder glowing light red pops upon the holo-screen.

“...and five targets have been select with a further five on standby.”

“Ok, choose one at random and take us to a hovering position.”

The Pungent Defiller speeds halfway around the planet to come to rest over a rather sad looking, pale structure.

“The humans call this ‘The White House’,” the computer informs you.

“Fucking hell,” you scoff, “I bet it took them ages to come up with that.” With a quick mental command you incinerate this pathetic ‘White House’ using the blue training death ray you would usually use for carving obscene symbols on asteroids.

“Next.” You command. The ship skips across a third of the planet before coming to a stop above another pale, pathetic structure, sitting within a drab, grey city of some sort.

“This one is known as Buckingham Palace,” says the computer. You decide to switch things up and use the acid beam on this so-called landmark, it melts in on itself and forms a small acid lake.

You cast a quick glance at the PCSA reading, expecting to see a dark red sphere, but instead a yellowish cube is displayed.

“There’s something wrong with the PCSA display,” you huff.

“Actually,” responds the computer, “it is running accurately. I’ve just run half a million test patterns to check - and it seems that the PCSA is currently medium."

"So by obliterating these two buildings I've actually improved the mood of the whole planet?"

"So it appears," says the computer, "But we need a third data point to confirm a clear correlation."

"Ok, what's next?"

The ship zooms across the planet again before coming to rest above another dreary looking city surrounding a slightly more interesting set of buildings.

"The Earth beings call this complex 'The Kremlin'"

"Lets see how much they like this one then," you ponder as you rain down superheated plasma on 'The Kremlin' and reduce it to a radioactive pile of sludge.

The PCSA is now a light yellow octahedron with small green flecks.

Either the Earthlings really hated these buildings or they are big fans of acid lakes and radioactive sludge.

If you want to continue on this confusingly popular rampage of violent obliteration. ***Go to page 101****.*

Or

If you want to quit while you are seemingly ahead. ***Go to page 34****.*

147

A TENTACLE UP - NOT A TENTACLE OUT

About three Earth 'months' later, you've just finished a long night of remote American town fly-bys and a chain of cow dissections across eastern Europe.

You call up the frail Gunther Weishaupt on the holo-screen, for an update.

"Ahh, commander Flooge," croaks the increasing frail Grand Prefect of the Brotherhood of Enlightenment.

"I'm looking at the conquest map, Gunther. I'm not seeing a lot of progress."

The conquest map shows outlines of the numerous nations of the Earth. Those under the complete control of the Brotherhood are filed in red, those as yet unconquered remain white. The map is almost entirely blank white.

"Really? I'm sure that Lichtenstein has fallen to our dark conspiracy since last we spoke and - hang on," someone hands him a slip of paper, "yes, it looks like the Faroe Islands are in the bag too."

Two tiny specks of red flash up on the conquest map. Pathetic.

"Your pitiful schemes are taking far too long, Earthling." You rage. "I am sorely tempted to laser the whole place to pieces. Have you got any idea how many crop circles I've done in your last Earth 'week'?"

"I pray for your patience, commander Flooge," creaks Gunther Weishaupt, "The Flemish speaking part of Belgium is within our grasp and then maybe even San Marino will fall to us… Of course if you were able to offer us some more… practical assistance then I'm sure we could hurry things along. Maybe have a crack at Peru, maybe even New Zealand"

"Silence!" You thunder, "you will receive no more assistance than agreed, pathetic human. How on Exkroll VII can I rely on you to permanently run this planet for me if I need to do everything for you? You must learn to conquer on your own two, strange biped 'feet'."

You close off the holo-call before you really lose your temper. You've got a load of planning to do for the next set of anal probe abductions on the list.

If you want to continue with the current plan and support the Brotherhood of Enlightenment as they covertly conquer the Earth in painfully small increments. ***Go to page 142****.*

Or

If you've wasted enough time on this bunch of backwards air breathers and you decide to risk leaving them to it while you go and get on with some more rewarding conquering. ***Go to page 70****.*

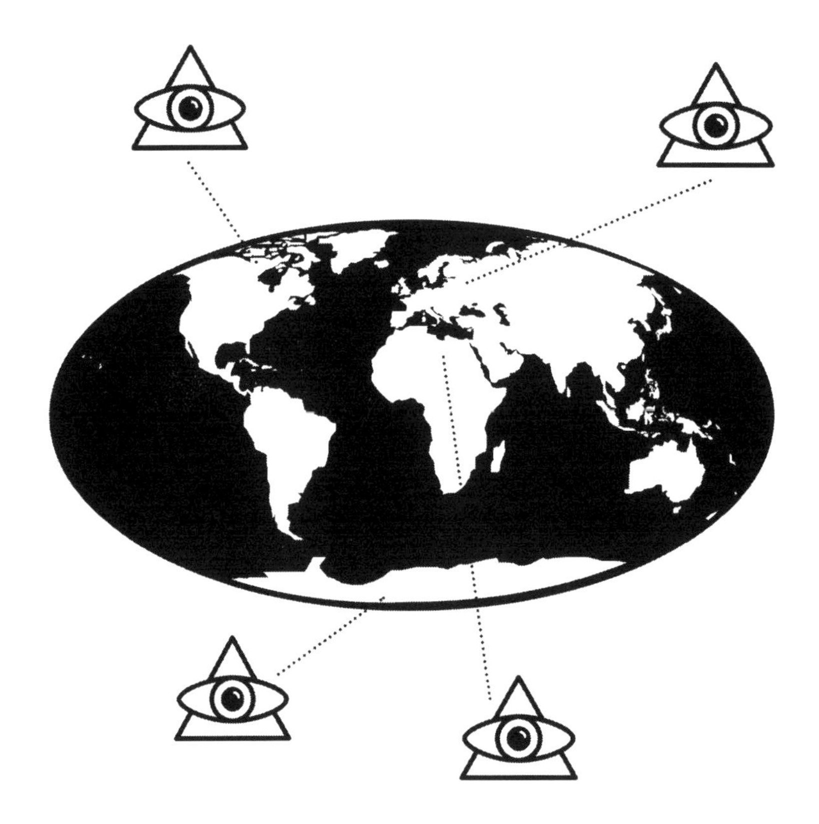

MAKE THE BEST OF A BAD JOB

As you know from earlier scans that there is at least some Trans-Cosmic Plastic lurking in the Earth's core, you calculate that you'd be better off scrapping the planet for parts at this point. Most of the surviving Earthlings are likely to be heavily irradiated at this point, which will liley make them ineffective slaves and almost certainly much less tasty.

You decide to use nuclear inversion missiles to effectively turn the planet inside out and allow you to harvest resources from the core.

The computer targets the optimum locations for the charges and then, with a wave of your dominant tentacle, the missiles are unleashed. Moments later the rocky lump of what is left of the Earth messily folds in on itself.

The glowing core of the planet is exposed and begins to solidify in the cold vacuum of space. In no time at all, everything that was the planet Earth now hangs in the void: a misshapen, grey-brown lump, its surface speckled with crystalline deposits of freeze-dried trans-cosmic plastic.

In fact, there's far, far more than you could expunge and transport aboard the Pungent Defiler.

If you decide to deploy a homing beacon for a GC mining crew to sort this out and then head back to head office. ***Go to page 12**.*

Or

If you want to safeguard your earnings by making multiple trips to transport the Trans-Cosmic Plastic to the nearest GC refinery, rather than relying on some dodgy mining crew. ***Go to page 16**.*

Or

If you realise that this is finally your chance to be rich, load up as much Trans-Cosmic Plastic as you can and sell it on the black market. ***Go to page 17**.*

150

VOLUNTARY APPRAISAL TRANSPORT

The dishy auditor seems surprised that you'd choose the appraisal option, but is as good as their word.

You are transported back to the Pungent Defiler, while a techno ray from the audit battle cruiser wipes all higher functions from the computer and sets an imperative auto-course back to GC headquarters.

So you are locked on a one way trip to take part in a potentially lethal workplace assessment, with no chance of escape, but at least the computer's been lobotomised. That really does cheer you up.

In an attempt to get you in the right frame of mind for the appraisal, you fill the travel tank with 'mellow yellow' stimulant fluid for and select a corporate motivational transport dream entitled '*Obliteration Memories*'.

As the ship begins to autonomously manoeuvre into a series of dimensional jumps you submerge yourself into the warm, yellow tank of slime and allow your brains to fill with a relaxing montage of burning cities and exploding moons...

You awake feeling extremely refreshed as The Pungent Defiler is coming into the main GC spacedock. There's a spring in your slither as you power cleanse off the transport fluid in the hygienarium and you feel almost abnormally confident as a purple transport beam buzzes into the ship and displaces you into the vast appraisal chamber. You just know you are going to nail this!

Go to page 75.

151

SLIM PICKINGS

You won't have much to show for it, but probably better to try and salvage what is left on the surface rather than incur the expense involved in blowing the whole planet up. You deploy a few enslavement drones and a couple of self building nanite factories to the bits of the planet where there are still significant parcels of population remaining.

It's such a low level of potential output that it is hardly worth your time to oversee things, so you dump a portion of the computer's AI core to keep an eye on the half a billion surviving Earthlings and see if it can work out something useful to do with them.

You fill out a post-conquer report, quantum beam it to GC headquarters and nervously await new orders.

The reply leaves you in no doubt that if you hadn't kept costs so low through the use of the interloper technique, then the profits from this mission wouldn't have covered the cost of your disintegration.

So, although they can't justify melting you down or even demoting you, management has decided that for the foreseeable future, you'll get nothing more challenging than planets populated by small rodents to conquer.

"So we're on Hamster Squad then?" Asks the computer, sounding pretty chippy about it.

"Shut up and put in a requisition for some sawdust bombs," you sneer.

Earth Conquering Status: You manipulated the Earth into nuking itself to near uselessness and as a result will be subjugating nothing more exciting than a Guinea Pig for the foreseeable future. Crucially though, you didn't get horribly killed.

GC Rank: Conqueror, level 3 ('Hamster Squad').

The End.

152

NOW THAT IS JUST TEXTBOOK CONQUERING

For the briefest moment you have a strange reluctance to transport back to the Pungent Defiler and bring your pleasant adventures in the being of Myra Eagleton to an end.

You quickly realise that these feelings may be the early onset of Alternative Personality Override, often known in the trade as 'going native'. You pull yourself together and quickly transmit: "Transfer me back at once," to the computer.

The purple haze of a transfer beam glows and the deck of your ship materializes before you as you reappear in the transformatication pod.

"Change me back. Change me back now!" You blurt at the computer. You can feel your atomic structure being realigned and in no time at all you are back in classic Flooge form.

The pod opens and you flop out into the floor, rapidly checking that all your favourite tentacles are intact and that your pleasure cavity is still entirely functional. Phew!

You stare in horror at the comatose form of the real Myra Eagleton, you can't believe that you seriously considered remaining in such a hideous biped form. You'd heard stories of conquerors going native (everyone's heard the cautionary tale of Taarl, the former conqueror and current Frog Deity), but you had never experienced it until now.

"Do you want me to freeze these human remains for transfer to R&D, Commander?" asks the computer.

"No, flush it into vacuum at once." You command.

With a small whooshing noise, the pod retracts into the ceiling and Myra Eagleton is fired into the void.

Earth is so bereft of any means of defense that you are able to conquer the planet entirely on automatic, using only the bare minimum of enslavement drones and AI nanite factory builders. You are able to leave the whole process to run itself while you catch up on the extended end-of-series special of '*Most Excruciating Space Whaling Accidents*' in the holo-lounge.

You are ejecting a very comfortable waste pellet in the hygienarium when the computer informs you that the Earth and its population are 100% conquered. Factory camps and resource mines have been set up across the planet - and a GC chef squad is on the way to evaluate whether the Earthlings should be farmed.

Thanks to the low-effort, cost effective way that you took over the Earth, in Cycles to come, performing a near-perfect, automated conquering will become known as 'Pulling a Flooge'.

Earth Conquering Status: You easily and efficiently conquered the Earth by spreading a message of peace and progress, then betrayed the entire civilisation for corporate profit and personal advancement. It really couldn't have gone any better.

Galactic Consolidated Rank: Promoted to Conqueror, level 2 with immediate effect and awarded 'Subjugator Of The DemiCycle'.

The End.

154

EPIC MONTAGE

There seems something just a bit off about this convoy, so you hang back and observe while a small swarm of your drones dive in to carry out a stealthy snatch protocol.

The drones have just located the MetaLitnium cargo and have begun relay transporting a small, but wildly valuable consignment back to your hold - when your instruments go crazy.

"Wowzers, looks like there's an ad-hoc dimension rift opening in this quadrant. Crazy scenes!" Cheers the computer.

A sparkling neon rift in space-time opens not far from the huge bulk of the GC freighter and an equally massive Star-Frigate bearing the markings of Universal Mercantile appears from hyperspace.

You're glad you held back, things are about to get messy, UM are GC's most hated corporate rival - they've been in open business war for longer than almost anyone can remember.

But rather than a violent scene of space battle, you watch as the GC escorts tractor beam a cargo container over to the UM frigate.

"Computer, monitor the comms between all ships," you snap.

"Hokey dokey, guvnor!" Pips the computer.

You merge into the ships' comms array in time to hear the GC ship announce, "OK, see you same time next OptiCycle," before the UM frigate disappears into another garish rift.

"Blimey - looks like we've stumbled onto some kind of intrigue and corruption. How delicious, how amazingly-" The computer goes quiet as you execute the holo-keystroke to suspend the amazingly annoying voice...

A few OptiCycles later, the PainBrungr hangs in the space near the GC corporate hyper rift, along with four automated gunships, purchased with the proceeds of your last haul.

As before, the GC freighter arrives and then shortly afterwards the same UM Frigate appears to relieve it of a cargo pod. This time, once the UM ship is safely back somewhere in sixth dimensional space, you swing towards the freighter. You task the automated gunships to take out the fighter escorts and then open a channel to the freighter captain and explain just how much cargo you will be taking in blackmail to avoid their ongoing treachery being reported back to GC management - then you move on to some more questions...

Within a single Cycle, you've assassinated the leaders of the entire Purple Moons Smuggling Conspiracy and established a base of operations for your nascent privateer armada on an abandoned casino asteroid.

From your, frankly rather chintzy, secret headquarters you begin a covert, heavily sub-contracted campaign of false flag attacks on both Galactic Consolidated and Universal Mercantile resources and interests. Pretty soon you have successfully seeded an all out pan-galactic corporate war.

As the forces of GC and UM knock lumps out of each other across at least five dimensions, your black market smuggling operation grows exponentially. Pretty soon you've upgraded from the abandoned casino asteroid to a modest snow planet out in the Eighth Quadrant.

While the attritional corporate battles are waging, you are quietly buying up heavily discounted stock in both of the mega-companies using a large array of shell corporations, dummy accounts and fake hedge funds. You now have multiple privateer armadas, covertly assisting or attacking the forces of either side in order to tip the balance of power and manipulate the cosmic stock market to your advantage.

With Galactic Consolidated on the brink of defeat and/or financial ruin, you are able to carry out a series of five million simultaneous and almost impossibly complex transactions, which realise and consolidate your total GC shareholding to a tiny fraction over fifty percent. You now have control of the company.

Using the considerable interest that you also hold in Universal Mercantile you are able to negotiate an immediate ceasefire without leaving your favourite Maskillion pleasure throne. Liquidating a tiny fraction of your UM holdings, you purchase a small personal fleet of Xarg-built Terror Barges and commission an army of Arachnian death-pirates to transport you to Galactic Consolidated headquarters to convene an extraordinary meeting of the board...

Your terrifying fleet snaps out of hyperspace near the colossal GC structure and heads to the exclusive docks of the atrium city where the top level GC employees live and work. You consider the irony that just twenty Cycles ago, a lowly conqueror such as yourself would have been summarily melted down for being this close to the glittering domes and crystalline skyscrapers of the atrium city - you decide to work through these complex feelings by lasering a few of the thousand storey skyscrapers into the void.

You eschew the GC transport beam for a heavily armoured motorized transport for the journey to the boardroom - you don't want the sneaky bastards on the board the chance to engineer some sort of accident. The hypertank rolls through the deserted streets of the atrium city, an elite squad of your Arachnian death-pirates manning all of the turrets.

In no time at all, you arrive at the Grand Administration Palace, then along with a small detachment of the most horror-inducing death-pirates, you head for the boardroom.

Go to page 140.

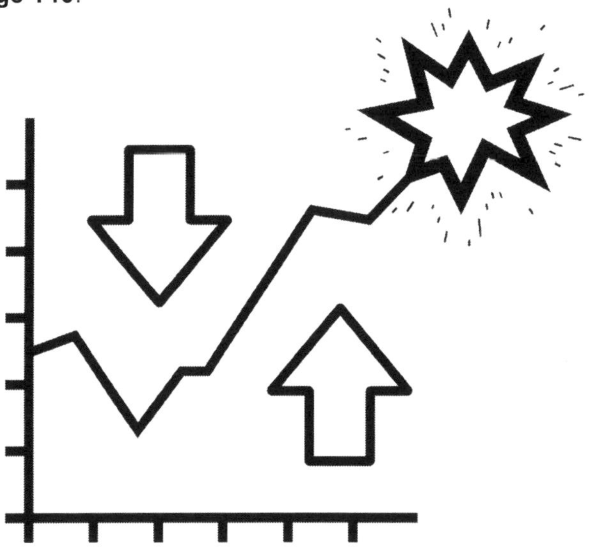

157

THE INEVITABLE ATTACK OF THE KILLER ROBOTS

By the time that the GC corporate navy was finally able to defeat the self replicating killer robot army that your mission to Earth spawned, at least two thousand star systems lay in ruins.

Not content with slaughtering the entire population of the planet in the twelve Earth 'minutes' after they were turned on, the metal murder machines quickly spread their campaign of terror across the stars with horrific efficiency.

Fortunately, you'd already assumed your original form back aboard the Pungent Defiler some time before what future historians will refer to as 'The Robocide Terror'.

Somewhat less fortunately, the GC hierarchy created a whole new sub-committee to come up with a punishment suitable enough for the death, damage and loss of profitability that they blamed entirely on you.

Without going into needless, graphic detail, the lengthy and unpleasant fate you suffered meant that 'Flooge' became colloquial slang in many different languages. It roughly translates as: "I feel like I've shat myself inside out."

Fame at last.

Earth Conquering Status: A rampaging mob of killer robots, with a hive intelligence based on the eccentric AI from your ship's computer, destroyed the earth along with a sizable chunk of the local sector of the galaxy.

Galactic Consolidated Rank: War criminal (executed with extreme prejudice).

The End.

158

LESSON LEARNT

Somehow, you just know that Colin and the Masters of Atlantis are going to be a complete let down and far more trouble than they are worth. Maybe it's that slight ache in your paranoia gland, maybe it's because of Colin's gold cape.

You cut off the call, set weapon aim for the lost land of Atlantis, but rather than lasering a channel through the rock, you use a heat ray to melt the seabed into a huge pool of lava which will should melt the tiresome fascists of Atlantis so they don't mess up any of your future plans.

"Most illuminating," creaks the voice of Grashbaq the wise. "Take note young students, of how Flooge correctly discerned the potential risk of engaging with the primitive and clearly incompetent Colin creature. A good conqueror must rely on their instincts at all times."

The holo-image of your old tutor turns to address you, "I knew you would provide an excellent example for study, Flooge. Alas we cannot continue to follow your next steps as this class has disintegrator training in a couple of MicroCycles. Farewell, my former student."

With that the holo-classroom fades out. You let out a burst of relief spray as you relax, glad that you didn't embarrass yourself in front of Grashbaq.

"Ok, computer," you think, "Put me in touch with this Brotherhood of Enlightenment."

Go to page 24.

159

TERMS AND CONDITIONS APPLY

It can't hurt to have a quick re-cap and check that the particle dribblers at head office haven't changed any major stuff while you've been in transit. A rumour has been going round that Captain Kaplonge from section eight was plunged into the star oven of Cpskilliom-V by the audit department after using the wrong form to submit fuel expenses.

Flicking an empty carton of Spice Irradiated Dark Matter off the desk, you punch in your authorisation codes and call up the file entitled *'Galactic Consolidated: Understanding Your Lethally Enforceable Contract (and Holiday Allowance)'.*

The left holo screen bursts into action, showing a montage of some classic planetary enslavements and solar absorptions while the Galactic Consolidate theme tune plays. You try to skip the intro, but it is unskippable and you receive a medium size electric shock to underscore this point. Eventually the following page of information appears, along with a rather shrill accompanying in-brain commentary.

Greetings [commander] - this summary information file is provided for your review in case of weak-minded uncertainty, auditory arbitration or transit related multiple brain failure.

Your contract with Galactic Consolidated stipulates the following objectives:

PRIMARY - Conquer your target planet/moon/comet/asteroid and secure available resources and/or population for the sole benefit of Galactic Consolidated.

SECONDARY - Ensure that no more than 50% of said resources or population are vapourised, de-dimensionalised, or otherwise rendered unusable during the conquering process.

TERTIARY - Avoid any and all loss of or damage to any GC assets and equipment.

Failure to achieve or exceed these targets or follow all corporate guidelines may result in GC rank demotion and/or an ad-hoc appraisal and/or a violently lethal corporate intervention.

The contract states that Galactic Consolidated will

A - Compensate your GC account according to the amount of usable chemical & mineral resources plundered.

B - Adjust your GC rank according to the amount of viable resources attained and/or slave labour/food provided by lifeforms subjugated.

C - If it becomes necessary, re-format your remains into an easily digestible paste to be enjoyed by your surviving clones/ colleagues.

((((Your holiday entitlement remaining in this cosmic Cycle is [15] CentiCycles - to be expunged no later than the Festivus of Krogon The Impatient.))))

Well, that all seems pretty much as you remember it - you have a quick sub-psychic flick through some supplementary files, just to double check on that expense thing and also to find the F2/987 form in order to make a pre-emptive workplace termination recommendation regarding Klurge.

You'd better check up on the planet "EARTH" that you've been assigned to conquer.

Go to page 7.

Printed in Great Britain
by Amazon